LORAMENDI'S STORY

A Lords of Shifters Novel

By Angela Carlie

To WLPL ~
Angela Carlie

Loramendi's Story

A Lords of Shifters Novel

Copyright 2011 by Angela Carlie

1st Edition: July, 2011

Cover design by Robin Ludwig Design, Inc.

One

Some think that space is the final frontier or something like that. Believe me, space has got nothing on what lives here on Earth. If people, the human type, could see what I've seen, they wouldn't be so afraid of aliens or the unknown of space anymore. Aliens are a walk in the park compared to the creatures biding their time to destroy—

Oh, wait. I'm getting ahead of myself. Let's start from the beginning.

Things started getting weird a few months ago when my best friend, Jess, arrived home from her trip to San Francisco. We lived in the same small town where I've always lived in the Columbia River Gorge—White Salmon, Washington. Windsurfing territory.

We hadn't been friends for very long. She had just moved to White Salmon about two years prior, but we immediately clicked like soul friends.

It was a late summer mid-afternoon when Jess' car squeaked into the driveway. The sound ran over the bird songs and wind chime music. Two dragonflies buzzed over my head before I darted from the brown grass and skipped over to the little red Honda, anticipating a big hug to leap from the vehicle.

The driver didn't look like my best friend, but on further examination, Jess sat behind the wheel with stranger hair.

"Oh my stars!" My jaw dropped. "What did you do?" I stepped closer and a smile crept onto my lips.

Resentment scribbled all over Jess' face. She opened the door and took her time crawling out of the car. "What?" Malice dissolved into a smirk with attitude. "You don't like my new look?"

"I don't know. Turn around. Let me see the whole thing."

She strutted, as if on a catwalk, and pivoted a quarter turn for my approval. She pushed one hip out with her hand on the other, puckering her lips in a serious pout. Her once long golden brown hair was now a short, pixie cut, dyed purplish red.

"You pierced your eyebrow!" Pink skin puckered around a silver barbell penetrating the outer edge of her right brow.

Jess poked her tongue out to reveal a stud straight through it as well. I gasped.

"You better close your mouth, Lora. Lots of bugs out." Jess pointed to the invisible bugs flying in the air.

I snapped my jaw shut.

Jess grabbed the bottom of her t-shirt and then laughed quietly to herself. "You like *that*? Well then, you will *love* these!" She winked and lifted her t-shirt for the world to see her creamy white boobs. Well, not the whole world, just me and possibly Old Man Franklin, the neighborhood snoop across the street.

I leaped two steps, yanked her shirt down, and made sure the old man wasn't having a heart attack in his front window. For once, he must have had better things to do.

"Your nipples too?" I whispered. This was not my best friend who left in June. The girl standing before me was a stranger who only resembled my best friend. "Why'd you do that?"

Jess didn't answer me with words, but only shrugged her shoulders as if to say she didn't know. She stuffed her hands into the pockets of her worn cut-off jeans. I twisted a long blade of grass between my toes. Words stuttered through my mind but they wouldn't form a sentence in my mouth. *Why isn't she talking? What happened to my best friend?*

"Do you want to sit down or what?" The way the question sliced through my mouth shocked me.

Jess shrugged again, her eyes never leaving the ground. "Sure."

I stomped toward the house and leaned against the handrail attached to the worn front porch. "So, are you going to tell me how your summer went or am I going to have to read your mind?"

Jess plopped onto the peeling white painted stairs. "I just hung out with my cousins a lot. We went to clubs on the weekends." She grinned. "No one ever asked for my ID. It was pretty cool and I met a lot of people. It's kinda weird coming back to this boring, lame town."

"I bet." My turn to roll eyes, but Jess wasn't even looking at me. She gazed up at the tree instead.

"I think I want to move there next year after we graduate," Jess said matter-of-fact like. "Maybe go to art school and live with my cousins."

"That sounds cool. There's one problem with that, though." I crossed my arms. "What about our plans to go to Seattle? I'm sure Seattle has just as many clubs if that's what you're concerned about." I turned away so she wouldn't see

3

the sting in my eyes betray me, because Jess didn't seem to care or remember the plans we had made before she left.

Jess snorted. "I always thought you only agreed to go with me to make me happy."

"No, stupid!" I forced a laugh and sighed with relief. "I wouldn't do *anything* just to make *you* happy. Who else would I want to escape this town with? There are absolutely zero cool people here other than us—oh and maybe Johnnie too."

Jess scrunched up her nose. "Did Johnnie find himself a girlfriend over the summer or am I gonna have to keep breaking his heart?"

"What do you think? He's still madly in love with the one and the only Jess!" My hands flew up in the air with dramatic sarcasm.

The wall between us crumbled a bit.

"Great." Her face vomited disgust.

"He's a fun guy. I don't see why you don't give him a chance."

She picked a brown and red leaf off the ground that had just fallen from the maple tree and ripped the flesh away from the spine, pretty much telling me that she was done talking about Johnnie.

I leaned closer to her, near her face, but she wouldn't look at me, flinch, or anything. "There were a ton of tourists and surfers in town this summer, more than usual anyway."

"Uggh...surfers." Jess never liked surfers. She claimed they were dirty and didn't have homes.

Dirty and homeless appealed to me, along with riling Jess up whenever she fell into these moods, which wasn't often.

"Quite a few hot ones too, I might add," I said.

A windsurfer didn't actually have to *be* hot to be dubbed as hot. All windsurfers were hot in my book. I didn't know why, but it had to do with the fact that they mastered a skill that scared the crap out of me. If only I could swim, then maybe I'd learn to windsurf.

Jess stared at a squirrel scurrying up the tree. It stopped at the lowest branch and twitched its tail several times before climbing higher. It disappeared into the abundance of leaves.

Behind Jess, a hairy spider strung webbing between two rose bushes in the garden to catch his dinner.

I tossed a small twig to get her attention. "We still going to the Bloody Pulp concert next week?"

"Why wouldn't we be?" she asked with heat in her voice.

I exhaled and figured she must be tired from the long trip home or something. She needed to chill with the attitude, though. "You want to go shopping before? I don't have anything to wear."

"I guess," she said.

"Sweet. I'll drive. We can go tomorrow if you're free..." I sprang to my feet. "Oh! I almost forgot something. Stay there a sec." The screen door snapped shut on rusty hinges behind me as I ran into the house and then thumped down the hall.

Jess loved photography. So much that I talked her into entering one of her photos at the state fair while she was away. It won second place.

I grabbed the red silk ribbon from my dresser. It flapped in my hand while I ran back down the hall. A car door slammed shut and an engine roared to life.

The little red Honda squeaked backwards, out of the driveway, and then sputtered down the road.

I stood at the door. Jess no longer sat on the stairs.

The maple tree continued to sway, shedding leaves onto the dry grass below it. Wind chimes sang once again in the distance. Across the street, in the large bay window of a small house, Old Man Franklin's face appeared—pale and shriveled, as always. He nodded toward me. I waved.

I began to turn away and then stopped, as did my heart. A shiver skipped across my arms. Jess' second place ribbon fell from my hand.

The light must have hit the glass pane in the door just right because at that moment a reflection of a face peered back at me, and it wasn't Old Man Franklin's.

And it wasn't mine.

Two

The reflection had my blond hair and my large brown eyes, but the high cheekbones, long chin and wrinkled skin definitely didn't belong to me.

I wasn't alone.

I whipped around, knocking the lamp next to me. It crashed to the ground.

The living room was empty.

I searched down the hall, Aubrey's small bedroom, my even smaller room, the bathroom. Nothing. The kitchen. Empty.

The clock on the dingy white walls in the kitchen ticked louder than usual. Water from the faucet plopped by droplets into an empty sink and echoed against stainless steel. Humming vibrated from the ancient olive green Frigidaire.

Color washed away from everything, like an old black and white movie. Previously beige countertops, green stove, dirty brown Linoleum floors, and faded yellow curtains all turned gray.

My heart thumped faster than usual, too. Normal left the room.

The screen door smacked shut. I jumped.

Normal returned.

My petite godmother, Aubrey, walked into the kitchen with an armload of groceries. She dumped them onto the very beige counter.

"Hey kiddo! Looks like the lamp got knocked over. Could you pick it up for me?"

I shook the chills away. The sturdy amber glass and brass lamp from 1970 wasn't broken, so I set it on the table and looked out the screen door. Old Man Franklin no longer stood in his window.

"How was your day?" Aubrey's voice boomed from the kitchen.

I walked back into the kitchen, sure that I must have imagined the reflection and stood at the beige counter. "Okay, I guess. Jess stopped by."

Aubrey had a look she gave me when she thought I wasn't telling the entire truth or when she didn't approve of something. Gravity pulled her chin down while her eyes peered at me over invisible rims. But, she didn't wear glasses, so it was rather funny whenever Aubrey gave me *the look*.

"You don't sound as happy as I'd expect. You've been sulking all summer long since she left. What's up?" Aubrey pulled a bag of red apples out and put them in the fridge.

I stepped behind her to help with the groceries. "She's just different. Something must have happened or maybe she thinks she's too cool for me now. I don't know. She wouldn't even tell me about her summer…just kind of shrugged it off like it was no big deal. Then, she totally took off without saying goodbye." Since Aubrey didn't move to let me help, I sat down at the little table. "Oh, and she cut her hair off!"

Aubrey's eyes bugged out.

"Yeppers, she cut it all off and got nipple rings and dyed her hair—"

"Wait a minute." Aubrey held her hand up. "Did you say nipple rings? As in she got her nipples pierced?"

"Yeah," I said, all drawn out.

"Wow, I've got to see that. I bet it hurt like a mother..." Aubrey glanced at me as if she realized what she said. "Well, maybe she's just going through a phase. I'm sure she'll grow out of it."

"Hmmm, maybe." I wasn't so sure. "We're going shopping in The Dalles tomorrow. Is it okay?"

"Yeah, that's fine." Aubrey picked her purse off the counter. "Are you driving? Will you need gas money?"

"I've got some tip money saved up for gas. It's been a boring summer, remember?"

The glimmer in Aubrey's brown eyes disappeared. "I know, hon. I'm sorry. The summer before senior year should have been the best yet. Maybe I can make it up to you sometime during the school year if I can get some vacation. Spring break or something?"

I nodded. "Cool."

My real mother disappeared when I was one year old and Aubrey took me in. They had been best friends since childhood. If Aubrey didn't have to care for me, she probably would have been married with her own kids by now. She always reassured me that we were meant to be and she wouldn't have it any other way, but her words never took the guilt away no matter how often she said them.

After we stuffed the cupboards with the groceries, Aubrey kicked back in her recliner, watched the evening news, and ate leftover pancakes. She looked as young as ever with her long brown hair pulled back into a ponytail, like she never aged. Ever. Seriously.

9

"I'm going to bed now," I said.

Her eyes remained focused on the TV. Her hand held the fork suspended in midair between the plate and her mouth.

"Hey, Aubrey?"

She snapped her head my direction. "Goodnight, hon."

"Night."

Morning came early the next day. The sun beamed and the birds chirped while I rushed up the trail to my favorite spot above our house. It was a warm morning—a good indication that the day would be a scorcher.

Normally I walked to the end of the trail, but only made it a quarter of the way that day before my legs wimped out. Besides, if I didn't start writing soon, my dream may have been lost forever. I sat on a giant rock to record my dream from the previous night.

I'd kept a journal for two years prior and filled it with the random and weird dreams that began to haunt me at about the same time.

***

Dream Journal Entry August 28th (more like nightmare):

The boy's crying was insufferable. The moans from his chest were soulful for someone so small, as if he carried the sins of the world on his shoulders. His deep clear eyes were stained red around the edges from the sorrow that seeped from them.

What could cause such sorrow in one so young? I wondered as his sobs seared my heart.

The boy of maybe only ten years sat on the cold, wet stone floor in the corner of what looked like a cellar when a man cracked the door open, allowing a stream of light to breach the darkness, blinding the boy.

"Stop that unbearable crying! You will wake your brother," the man said.

The weeping stopped instantly, but only for a moment

The man slammed the heavy wooden door the remainder of the way open against the wall as he entered, walking with long strides in his massive leather boots to the corner where the boy sat. He hovered over the boy, darkening the corner again.

I scanned the room in a panic for someone or something to help the boy. "Someone help!" I shouted, but no sound came from me—only thoughts. I was a mere witness to this maddening nightmare.

The man gazed down at the boy and his expression softened. "Why must you continue with this suffering, Xifan? Your brother is adapting just fine, yet you sit here still crying!" The anger in the man's voice was restrained. He bent down, touching the boy's face. "It pains your mother that you must behave this way." The man seemed conflicted.

"I'm sorry, Father." The boy's lips curled downward, his blue bloodshot eyes seeped pain. "The voices pierce my mind—it hurts so much, Father." The crying continued. The boy clutched his knees to his chest.

The man stood from his crouched position, crossed his arms in front of him, and stared at the boy for several minutes, thinking.

The sobs seethed louder and he pleaded, "I'm so sorry, Father. Make the pain go away, please!"

The man's face contorted into a painful grimace. His body became rigid. The muscles in his neck protruded and grew thick. Finally, he renounced his internal war with a loud bellow. His body twisted unnaturally. All went silent for

11

a split moment until the once-was-man roared the blood curdling sound of a giant grizzly bear.

The lackluster expression on the boy's face exposed an understanding. The bear turned on all fours and left.

When the door closed behind the bear, the boy screamed in the dark silence of his cell.

Three

The gas station hopped with people rushing in and out of the small convenience store, their hands filled with coffee, munchies, and lottery tickets, ready to start Monday. I pulled my antique, maroon Datsun to the gas pump, filled the tank and then stepped inside the store to buy a pack of gum.

The most beautiful guy ever held a giant bottle of water in his hand and stood frozen like a statue in the gum aisle. He looked like one of those cardboard advertisements—all supermodel like. Seriously, he was *that* hot. His warm clear eyes burned a hole through my heart. His strong jaw clenched as if he concentrated. Maybe he was thinking what he wanted to buy. I laughed to myself. Sometimes the variety in convenience stores could be overwhelming.

He kept glancing at me. He didn't move out of the narrow aisle to let me pass.

A musky, earth-like scent emanated from him that stirred my senses. It was so yummy. I tried to smile, but my face wouldn't obey my brain. Heat rose up my neck and prickled my ears. Finally, my legs moved past the gum aisle, and I hid in the chip aisle, allowing enough time for the hottest guy in the world to leave.

After a minute, I snuck a glance around the corner. He no longer advertised the beauty of statues and bottled water, and must have left the store because only a light scent lingered.

When I drove out of the parking lot, he stood on the corner watching me. I must have had a mile long booger hanging from my nose because guys never noticed me, let alone hot guys. Maybe my hair had gunk in it or something. I checked for nasal secretions and hair bugs in the mirror. Nothing.

People passed through town all the time so I didn't think I'd ever see him again.

Jess' mom's car sat in the driveway when I pulled up to their house. Mandy had usually left by then. She owned a small art gallery in nearby Bingen, an even smaller town than White Salmon. So, instead of blaring on the horn as was tradition, I opted to go up to the door to be polite.

"Please don't let Amy be home," I said to the air before reaching the door. Amy, Mandy's sister, creeped me out because she stared at walls and sometimes hummed under her breath. She never really had anything important to say and it became painful to be stuck in a room with her for any period of time.

The single level mid 1900's style house screamed Frank Lloyd Wright. I learned in art history class he invented craftsman style houses or something like that. It had very simple straight lines, lots of dark wood and leaded glass throughout. There weren't many houses like it in town.

Mandy opened the door with her arms stretched out for a hug before I could knock. "Good morning, Lora!" She held her long, brown hair pulled back in a barrette and wore black, as always. Laugh lines caressed her pale eyes.

"Hi. Morning." Unnatural cheer coated my voice. She almost squeezed the life out of me.

"Jess is getting ready. Come in and have a seat in the living room if you want." Mandy waved her hand for me to come in. She closed the door behind me.

All kinds of random, dark pieces of furniture speckled the interior. Large windows on the south side of the home framed spectacular views of the Gorge. From the living room, the Hood River Bridge over the Columbia River connecting Washington and Oregon filled the framed glass. The windows let in a ton of light, so unless it was dark outside, they rarely needed lights. Even then, they used only small lamps that emanated a warm glow.

Amy sat in the living room on the leather couch. Wonderful.

"Hey there, Amy," I said.

She stared at the flames popping in the giant rock fireplace, which was weird on such a warm morning. Her short blond hair, which usually held the entire stock of Walgreen's gel and mousse to create a spiked platform atop her head, fell limp and wet.

"So, uh, how are ya?" I asked.

"Fine." Amy's voice cracked. She bit her lip and then turned her head toward the windows.

Jess walked in. Her new purplish short hair also had a streak of green in front that I hadn't noticed the day before. It reminded me of an emo cartoon I'd seen commercials for.

"Are you *finally* ready to go?" I asked.

"Yeah, let's go. See ya, Mom. Amy."

Amy didn't turn her head away from the flames, just waved her hand in the air and wiped her face on the sleeve of her other arm.

"Bye girls, you be safe!" Mandy shouted after us before we closed the door.

"You saved me. I almost had to talk to Amy." I jumped into the car and slammed the heavy, solid door to make sure it latched. "So why did you just take off without saying bye yesterday?" I drove down the road.

Jess shrugged and smacked her gum. "Old Man Franklin was freaking me out. Besides, I forgot I had something to take care of."

"And?" I asked.

"And what? That's it."

"Whatever." I rolled down my window. Jess was never one to elaborate on anything, even if I did deserve an explanation. "So, why is Mandy home? I thought she usually opens up the gallery at eight."

"It's a long story and kind of weird." Jess shrugged and then blew a small bubble from the pink gum, popping it and snapping it back into her mouth.

"Okay. We have half an hour until we get to The Dalles. So spill." I drove toward the bridge into Oregon.

Jess turned in the front seat to face me, oddly eager to talk all of a sudden. "So, Amy was working at the logging site yesterday and one of the guys on her team got tore up pretty bad by some wild animals." Her voice went weak at the end. I glanced over. She wore a mangled expression on her face and reached to turn down the radio.

"Seriously?" I asked. "Is that what was wrong with you yesterday?"

Jess nodded, but I couldn't tell if she was answering my question or just moving her head. "Anyway, Amy said that they were walking out to where they usually meet the rest of

16

the crew when out of nowhere a bunch of animals just pounced on the guy." Jess cracked her window. "It wasn't just a lone wolf or a bear, but a few wolves and a giant bear, like, working together. Totally weird."

"Oh my stars! Did Amy get hurt?" I asked.

"That's the freaky part." Jess shuddered. "Amy just froze. She couldn't do anything but scream, and she couldn't even do that until the guy was half eaten. She was, like, so terrified that her body wouldn't work—she tried to run but her legs wouldn't move.

"Amy said the bear looked at her and then nodded. It wasn't until it nodded at her that she could scream for help. But by then, the animals had run off and the guy was in pieces all over the place. They didn't even touch Amy."

"What the heck?" I said when Jess stopped for air. "That's weird. Does Amy taste bad or something?"

Jess shrugged. "I know, right? My mom went to pick her up at the police station last night and Amy had blood splattered all over her—she was pale as a ghost."

Quiet spread over the car. I couldn't believe what Jess had just told me. Nothing like that had ever happened before. A couple years ago, some random hunter accidentally got shot and killed, but that's the only weird death in the forest that I could remember. They had a town meeting about gun safety a month after that accident. Not that I went or anything, but yellow flyers advertising the meeting were posted in every store window in town.

We reached the end of the bridge and paid the dollar toll to pass into Oregon before merging onto the freeway.

"Do you know who the guy that, eh… you know, was?" I asked.

"No. Amy won't tell us until the police have a chance to contact the guy's family. He's not from here though. He was here making some extra cash for the summer."

Not a local. Good. That would have sucked if a local got killed. The fact that he wasn't a local made me a little suspicious, though. Jess liked to make up stories and this sounded like a big, giant, weird story.

"I hope Amy is going to be okay," was all I could say. Jess nodded in agreement.

***

The thing I hated most about shopping was nobody ever had any clothes I liked. Shopping sucked. I was seriously picky about my clothes. They needed to be nonconforming and fit just right, thus making it even more difficult. My body wasn't shaped normal, I guess. Normal people must not have had short legs. Jess didn't have that problem. She'd go into one store and find everything she needed. I, on the other hand, took all day just to find one pair of jeans.

We walked across the street through the sweltering heat to the billionth store. Mannequins wearing coordinated outfits stared down at us while we meandered through the aisles.

I found several shirts, a couple sweaters, and even a pair of jeans that I needed to try on. Jess found a pair of skater shorts that she tried on and didn't even let me see how they looked on her. She crashed on the fluffy couch in front of my dressing room while I finished.

With the last t-shirt and pair of jeans on, I stepped out and modeled for Jess. She gave me a wink of approval, which finalized my decision to purchase everything. Thank the universe; shopping was over.

Back in the dressing room, I peeled off the jeans and t-shirt. My stomach rumbled. "Hey, you hungry?" I asked the air and turned to face the door.

Jess stood in the half-opened doorway of the dressing room. Her jaw relaxed and her twinkling eyes traveled from my hips to my face in a blink of a second and made me feel like a giant piece of chocolate cake with ice cream on top, and sprinkles on top of that.

"Oh my stars, Jess!" I jumped a foot into the air. Jess jerked out of her cake monster stare, blushed, and turned away. "You scared the crap out of me." I pushed the door.

"Oh, sorry. I was just closing the door because it...uh...had opened." Jess stammered.

I questioned myself about what just happened. Jess wouldn't feel *that* way about me. No way. The tense air lingered in the confined dressing room. I took a few slow breaths, so Jess wouldn't hear me, and sat down on the stool for a moment to push away those thoughts and the image of Jess' seductive look. An alarm rang within my chest. Not an alarm of danger, but one that warned me a transition was near, change was coming. Or it had already arrived. Jess changed, and so did our relationship. No. I didn't want to believe that just happened. The door simply opened and she was just shutting it. Not watching me dress.

With a smile on my face as stiff as the mannequins', I headed for the cashier where Jess waited. She held her bag and avoided eye contact by looking at her feet instead.

I paid for my stuff and stepped toward her with the same plastic expression. "Hey, are you hungry?" I managed to squeak out.

"Sure." She shrugged with zero expression, like a blank piece of paper.

"'Kay. Let's go to that pizza place." I pointed to the brick building about a block down the street.

Outside felt more like a dry sauna than the outdoors. Even the pavement burned through my sandals.

Two of White Salmon High's elite walked toward us. Oh great. I poked Jess in the ribs and nodded toward the soon-to-be-invasion-of-peace. A grumble escaped her mouth and she rolled her eyes.

Dani's and Rachael's confidence moved along with their strides, their heads held high and hipster-wannabe attitudes. The thing we hated most about the hipster-wannabes, which is a label only Jess and I knew of, was their horrible acting ability. Pretending not to be rich didn't go over real well with us kids that weren't rich. Well, Rachael's family wasn't as rich as Dani's, so she fit into the hipster-wannabe group not by definition, but by her attempts at acting like she did. We felt that since she tried so hard, we might as well award her the title, too.

Dani seemed to set the rhythm of their steps with her blond ponytail swaying back and forth, back and forth, while she walked. Rachael stayed with the pace, but with a smooth stride, like a dancer, that kept every one of her light-brown hairs in place.

They yelled out our names and waved their hands over their heads in our direction.

"Just keep your head low and walk fast. Pretend we don't see them," I mumbled, just loud enough for Jess to hear me.

Jess obeyed and we ducked into the pizza restaurant. "Safe!" we said under our breath. The doors swung closed behind us. We spoke too soon because just as we got up to the counter, Dani and Rachael skipped through the doors with their Urban Outfitter bags in hands.

"Hey you guys!" Dani said. "Didn't you hear us yelling for you?"

"No. Where were you?" Jess asked.

"Never mind." Dani shrugged her shoulders in an 'oh well' kind of way and tilted her head like a puppy trying to understand. "How are you guys? I haven't seen you all summer! Hasn't it been just the best summer *ever?*"

"Yeah, great." I turned to the reader board to figure out my lunch options.

"Aren't you excited to be going back to school as seniors this year? It's going to be exciting! Have you gotten your schedules yet? I wonder if we're going to be in any classes together." Dani rambled on and on.

Jess rolled her eyes and I released a heavy sigh.

I read the menu above the cashier while Dani continued to talk to the air. I ordered the veggie pizza slice with a salad and soda and took my tray to a table by the front windows. The thought crossed my mind to sit at a table for two so Dani and Rachael couldn't sit with us. I debated for a moment. Then I sat at the larger table for all four of us. Sometimes I hated my soft side.

Everyone else ordered pepperoni pizza slices instead of veggie. When they sat down, Dani jabbered on as if everyone listened, about unimportant stuff like homecoming and the senior graduation party.

21

Jess glanced at me out of the corner of her eye. Humor etched across her face. All the vibes and weirdness from the dressing room had long vanished and we gobbled our pizza as fast as possible.

"Have you noticed all the hot windsurfers in town this summer?" Rachael finally got a word in when Dani forked salad into her mouth.

"See Jess! I told you!" I said. "Oh, and I saw one of them this morning at the gas station. He was the hottest guy I've ever seen. Even though he stared at me a little bit too much." I shrugged. "Did you meet anyone this summer, Rachael?"

"Uh, no." Rachael laughed. "Dani did though."

Dani scrunched up her face in protest. "No I didn't!" But then her eyes beamed rainbows when Rachael continued.

"Yes, you did." Rachael looked at us. "Dani flirts with him every time she goes down to the river. She says she's going there to lie in the sun, but we all know she's going down there to ogle at the hot windsurfer. I don't blame her though, he's totally fine."

"Does this guy like you, Dani?" I asked. I loved windsurfers and if he was hot, he deserved my attention. Of course I wouldn't ever talk to the guy. I wasn't brave enough, but I could look. "You should introduce him to us. Oh, and how about introducing him to Jason, too. Shouldn't he be back from his trip this week?"

"Don't worry about Jason," Dani said. "We broke up."

Jess' mouth dropped open before mine. We sat there for a split second comprehending what she just said. Dani and Jason had been an item since elementary school. They were never apart for a very long time. If they truly broke up, the world must be turning the wrong direction, because no one fathomed this could ever happen.

"Don't look at me like that!" Dani flinched. "It wasn't my idea. He wanted to see other people while he was gone. Like anyone else would put up with his sorry ass. So I said fine and that's that."

I set my fork down. "I'm sure Jason will be totally jealous of this windsurfer guy and beg for you to get back together with him. Where is he from? Is he staying here? How old is he? Are you and this guy serious? When can we meet him?" I'm not normally a person who cares about other people's gossip, but, like I said, a hot windsurfer usually made for nice eye candy. Especially the mysterious types who surfed here for the summer and then disappeared forever.

"Actually, no. To everything," Dani almost whispered. "He doesn't really know that I exist." She scratched her arm and stared at her salad. "I tripped once on the beach and he helped me up. He was super nice and introduced himself. That was the only time he spoke to me."

I had never seen Dani Towner like that. The world definitely changed that summer. Dani, the most superficial person I'd ever met in my entire life, showed a new side, one that didn't fit her.

"Oh, well." I took a sip from my soda. "He's probably some psycho anyway. Things always happen for a reason and if you were meant to date him, then you will."

Jess rolled her eyes. She squirmed in her chair and picked at the lettuce on her plate.

We finished eating and said goodbye to Rachael and Dani. Once inside the car, the heavy air returned. Jess stared out her window. I clicked on the radio for the trip home.

I turned onto the I-84 West ramp and pushed the gas pedal to the floor. My old Datsun barely hit 35 mph when a dark mass of fur jumped from the trees onto the shoulder of the ramp several feet ahead.

I eased off the gas and squeezed the steering wheel. "What the...Jess, look!" The giant bear turned its head. Two menacing blue eyes glared as we approached.

"Oh my god." Jess gripped the dashboard. "What kind of bear is that?"

We rolled closer to the bear. It didn't move. The closer we got, the bigger it seemed—almost as tall as the car.

Jess rolled up her window. "I wonder if it's that same bear Amy saw."

"Have you ever seen a bear with blue eyes before?" Blue eyes were not a normal attribute for bears as far as I knew. But then, the only bears I'd ever seen were at the Oregon Zoo, and they had black eyes. Not blue.

"Nope," Jess said "Maybe we should speed up to pass it." She looked behind us. "Those idiots behind us probably won't let us back off the ramp."

A loud horn blared. In my rearview mirror, a car inched along with us, way too close to our bumper. The bear stood on its hind legs. It towered us with ginormous paws clawing at the air. I cranked my head down to see its face through the windshield, but it was too tall.

"Um, yeah, we better speed up!" Jess latched her hands around her seat belt, as if that would protect her.

I stepped on the gas but, my old car burped in protest and took its time accelerating.

The bear growled, landed back on all fours and trotted next to the car.

Adrenaline pulsed through me and my foot pressed the gas pedal as far as it would go. Every muscle in my body turned to stone. "Oh my god, oh my god, oh my god!" I restrained the scream trying to escape my throat.

The bear, running on all fours, kinked his neck so his blue eyes pointed directly at me through the passenger door window. His shiny black nose twitched; foam flew off his lips.

Jess scurried onto the middle console, stretching her seatbelt, and leaned onto me, getting as far away from the door as possible. "Go, go, go, go! Faster!"

"I'm trying!" I pounded on the steering wheel because that would obviously help us speed up. When my Datsun finally reached 40, the bear slowed down. We sped up and merged onto the freeway. I caught my breath. The stupid car that honked his horn, making the bear freak out, sped past us and honked one last time to let us know how he felt. In the mirror, the crazy bear stood on the shoulder, watching us drive off as if we were leaving behind a friend.

Jess met my eyes with hers, which could have popped out of her face at any moment. We both burst into relieved laughter.

"Oh my stars! That was just... I don't even know...Just weird!" I said.

"I know, right?" Jess turned to face the rear window.

"Loramendi!" A man's voice hollered.

I turned to Jess. She continued to watch behind us. "Did you hear that?" I asked.

"What?" Jess glanced at me, her right eyebrow arched.

"Someone said Loramendi."

"No. What are you talking about?" She scrunched up her face.

"I thought I heard a voice say 'Loramendi.' Maybe it was on the radio or something." I shrugged. It wasn't the radio, though. The name came from within my head, not my ears. Just like the dreams, the reflections, the color disappearing from everything, and now voices. Maybe I was getting sick. Sick in the head.

I shook away the weirdness.

The drive home was as beautiful as the morning trip, but hotter. Summers got pretty dang hot in the Gorge, but I guess that's the price to pay for living in such a place. We became tiny bugs driving in a not-much-larger car down the highway with the cliffs towering above us on one side and the river rushing next to us on the other.

We pulled up to Jess' house. She opened the door. "See ya next week, I guess."

"Hey, me and Johnnie are going hiking," I said. "Do you want to go?"

"Sure."

"Johnnie's going to pick me up at ten. We can pick you up after that, if that's cool with you. There's a big waterfall on this one. You'll love it!"

"Cool. See ya then." Jess shut the door.

I drove home up the hill.

Fans blew the air around my house and all the drapes had been pulled closed to keep the hot sun from entering our sanctuary. Perfect.

I threw my bags onto the floor of my room next to a pile of dirty laundry that needed some attention and stripped down to a t-shirt and underwear. I crawled into my soft bed. The cool sheets draped over my warm skin, and the steady rhythm of the fans soothed my mind. My eyes grew heavy. The image of the bear running along the car burned the back of my eyelids. Fog came fast, drifting toward me and all around me.

As I wandered in the fog, a car horn, of all things, rang far off in the distance. The sound sped closer and closer. The fog shrank. It became so light that I saw green tree branches a foot in front of my face.

The horn seemed angry and long.

I jolted awake.

Four

My eyes adjusted and focused on rays of sunlight pouring in from the side of the red drapes and the dust dancing in the air before I saw the time on the clock. 10:05 AM.

I jumped out of bed and stumbled out of my room. My legs tingled and buckled under me, but managed to get me to the front door. Johnnie sat in his little yellow pickup. His arms flew into the air when he saw me and he yelled out his window, "What the heck, Lora! Why aren't you dressed?"

Cool air hit my bare legs. I pulled my t-shirt to cover my underwear and leapt behind the door, then popped my head out from the side. "My alarm didn't go off. Jeez. Come in for a few minutes. Okay?"

Johnnie turned off the truck's engine. I ran down the hall to put some clean clothes on and freshen up in the bathroom. I grabbed the worn jeans draped on my desk chair and a blue t-shirt from the dresser drawer. The TV clicked on in the living room.

I combed my hair, then pulled it back in a ponytail, brushed my teeth, washed my face, dabbed on deodorant, and dashed out of the bathroom in record time.

Grabbing an apple out of the fruit basket and a bagel out of the bread box in the kitchen, I yelled for Johnnie. "Let's go!"

His head snapped away from the TV and toward me. "Wow. That was fast."

I slid into the tiny seating area behind the bucket seats of Johnnie's little King Cab pickup so Jess could sit in the front with Johnnie. He reached to open the rear window— probably remembering my mild case of claustrophobia.

Jess sat on the swinging bench on the porch we stained for her mom last summer. She took her time walking the short distance to reach us and then jumped into the passenger seat.

"Hey Jess!" Johnnie's eyes lit up.

"You're late." She glanced back at me with a smirk on her face before turning to Johnnie. "Aren't you just full of sunshine this morning? Nice haircut."

I forgot to tell Jess this bit of gossip. Johnnie always had long blond hair that he pulled back into a ponytail. One day early that summer, he chopped it off. He looked better with it short.

"Me? Look at you." Johnnie said. "You're an entirely different person." He flashed his pearly whites. "I like it."

"Did you miss me?" Jess asked with whine.

"You know I did. Life is boring here without you. You should never leave again." Johnnie's voice dripped with sarcasm. He pushed Jess playfully and she punched him hard.

"Hey! I was here." I hit Johnnie on the back of his head.

"Stop hitting me! You know what I mean. You were just as bored."

"Yeah, I suppose." I rolled my eyes.

"How far is the trailhead from here?" Jess asked.

"About a twenty minute drive west on I-84," Johnnie said.

Forty-five minutes later, we pulled into the parking lot to the trailhead and parked close to the trail signs. Johnnie must not have accounted for the lost time from driving his old pickup; it barely did fifty-five miles per hour.

He grabbed his backpack from the bed of the truck. Jess took her camera out of her bag and hung it around her neck. She snapped photos almost immediately—mostly of Johnnie and me.

The clouds trapped the hot, muggy air. It stuck to my skin and clothes.

Thick evergreen trees rose up into the sky forever. Lush vegetation grew abundantly all over the floor of the forest, but the trail was clear so we didn't worry about poison oak as long as we didn't stray from it.

After about a mile and a half into the hike, past several creeks and ponds, we came to one of the first waterfalls, Metlako Falls, and paused for a few photos. We crossed the bridge over Sorenson Creek and hiked until we reached Punch Bowl Falls, which is world famous for breathtaking views and is featured in many calendars. I read this tidbit from our trail guide. The whitewater flowed from a steep, mossy cliff into a pristine emerald pool deep in the canyon, creating a punch bowl. The entire spectrum of green lined the rock walls.

"Should we stop here to eat?" I asked. "I'm kind of hungry and I don't really want to go much further because the heights are a little crazy."

Johnnie and I had gone further the last time we hiked here. The wet, slippery trail etched out of the stone wall scared the crap out of me. I had clung to the side of the rock,

30

inching my way to the end of the trail. I didn't really want to deal with that anxiety again.

"Are you sure you don't want to go further, Lora?" Johnnie winked. He probably remembered how much I flipped out last time.

"I'm absolutely sure, thank you very much."

Johnnie laughed. "Let's sit over there." He pointed to a cove next to the turnout by the falls.

We sat on the rocks and Johnnie handed us each a sandwich and bottle of water.

"Thanks, Johnnie," I said.

"Look at you. All domestic and stuff." Jess grinned. "Thanks." She grabbed the food from him.

"Did you get any cool pictures yet?" Johnnie asked.

"I think so," Jess answered. "How could I not? This trail is awesome. I can't believe I haven't been on this one before."

"I know, huh?" Little pieces of bread flew out of my mouth.

"Eww, Lora. You're gross!" Johnnie leaned away.

"I know, huh?" I laughed out again.

We finished our sandwiches and Johnnie went on a bit further. Jess and I stayed back until he returned.

"Let me see the pictures you took today." I grabbed Jess' camera from around her neck and viewed the digital shots from the screen on the back.

"I think I got some pretty cool ones of that first falls we stopped at. Oh, look at this one I got of you and Johnnie." Jess leaned closer to me and pushed the button that scrolled through the pictures until she found the one she was looking for. Johnnie and I peered from behind the screen. My eyes rolled to one side and my tongue stuck out while Johnnie scrunched his face like he just bit into a lemon.

"Oh my stars!" I laughed. "You have to delete—" Jess inched forward, her lips headed for mine. I jerked my head back before her lips got to me. I stopped laughing. We stared at each other for a split second. Invisible electric waves crashed into me before she pulled away.

"I'm so sorry," Jess whispered. She stood and walked back the way we came, looking at the ground.

I didn't move. My best friend tried to kiss me. Not a friendly kiss hello or goodbye, but a full-on, lip-on-lip kiss. The rock fell from underneath me. Curling my legs up to my body, I laid my head on my knees and wrapped my arms around them.

That was the second time in two days something like that happened. Never had this happened since I knew Jess before she went on her trip. Why did she now try to make our relationship something that it wasn't?

Sleep teased my eyes, so I closed them and waited for Johnnie to return and tried to forget about everything. I concentrated on the gushing water of the falls, the birds tweeting in the bushes, and the whooshing of tall evergreens swaying in the breeze.

"Loramendi!" a hushed man's voice said from behind me.

I jolted up and glanced to the bushes, finding only ferns and foliage. I strained to listen. The falls almost drowned the sounds of everything else.

It must have been a dream. An eerie feeling crawled up my spine that someone was watching me.

"Johnnie?" I hollered into the trees. "Is someone there?"

I scanned the trees, struggling to see through the thick ferns. Nothing—just my imagination. I sat back down.

Johnnie returned several minutes later, skipping and shouting that we needed to come with him and endanger our lives on the cliff to see the next falls. When he got to me, his eyes darted back and forth. "Hey, where'd she go?" Concern crept onto his face.

"She wasn't feeling very well. So she headed back to the truck. We should probably go take her home now."

"Oh, man. I hope it wasn't the sandwich," Johnnie said.

"No, she just has a headache I think." We hiked to the trailhead.

Jess lay on her back with her arms draped over her face in the bed when we got there.

"I told Johnnie about your headache, Jess. We're going to go home now."

She sat up without a word and crawled behind the passenger seat.

Johnnie jabbered about going hiking again this autumn when the leaves started to turn colors. I watched the world go by in a blur through the side window, not paying much attention to Johnnie because I concentrated on not blowing up. The tension between me and Jess wrung my guts and twisted my heart. I couldn't believe Johnnie didn't notice. I wanted to scream.

Something big moved in the trees. We drove by so fast I didn't have a chance to look twice—I tried. The sudden fog in the forest made it difficult to see. My head snapped back. I searched for whatever it was, but didn't find it.

The truck screeched and skidded. We slid sideways. My nose and cheek smashed into the window. We spun once, twice, three times in the center of the freeway and came to a stop.

Five

We faced traffic head-on. Cars zipped around us. A silver Mazda turned just in time to avoid colliding into us.

Skidding tires, crumpling metal, and broken glass thundered from behind us.

We sat for several silent moments, stunned and waiting for the traffic in front of us to completely stop. It finally did.

My nose twitched from the thick iron smell in the air. It grew stronger every second and coated my tongue with metallic seasonings. My stomach rumbled. "What's that smell?"

Johnnie and Jess sniffed.

"I don't smell anything." Johnnie stuffed his nose in his armpit. "It's not me!"

"What's it smell like?" Jess asked.

"I dunno. Like rust or something, maybe. It's hard to explain."

Johnnie turned the pickup around and drove it to the side of the road. Five cars lay crumpled facing various directions in front of us. Three lifeless deer claimed the middle of the freeway. Several more hobbled and crawled, trying to get away. Blood covered everything.

I dashed out of the pickup, not knowing why or what I could possibly do to help. The pounding of my heart thumped out all other sounds. I ran to the closest car. The windshield was smashed and the hood was caved-in.

"Is everyone all right?" My voice sounded faraway.

The woman sitting in the passenger seat with glazed eyes nodded. "I think so."

Johnnie bolted to the next car and other people zipped around too.

I stopped. The deer closest to me bellowed an agonizing scream. Her front legs squirmed to lift her body while her squished rear end kept her anchored to the ground. My panic switched to helplessness.

I couldn't breathe.

The deer's dark eyes locked with mine and she stopped bellowing. I forced myself to move forward, one step then two steps, until I reached her. Foam seeped from the corners of her small mouth. Her black, wet nose flared with breath. She laid her head on the ground between her front twig-like legs. Everything else sounded muffled, like I had cotton in my ears, except for her heavy breaths.

Tears blurred my vision and burned down my face. The inside of my nose stung. I was helpless. It was hopeless. I wanted her suffering to end.

I touched the top of her head. The beige fur felt coarse on the tips of my fingers. She exhaled, blinked, and then her entire body relaxed. I waited for her chest to rise again. It never did.

My hands went numb, my arms tingled, my heart grew cold. I stood to leave the creature now at peace and turned to find three more deer screaming. Their blood formed puddles in the road.

I somehow found my breath. "They aren't dead! Help them! Somebody help them!"

My body crumpled in the middle of the road. "Help them." I couldn't pull my eyes away from the animals dying painfully in front of me.

Jess appeared at my side and put her arm around me. A large man wearing dirt covered denim overalls, a ball cap on his head, and a rifle in his hands walked past me. A loud bang and then blood splattered his overalls. I jumped and covered my ears. I kept them covered until he finished shooting each suffering deer.

Jess helped me up and we walked back to the pickup.

Two state troopers pulled along the side of the freeway and the clean up began.

Jess crawled into the back seat. I sat in the front, staring out the window into the forest at nothing but green life. Trees and bushes watched the workings of the world from their rooted homes without a word to say. About twenty minutes passed.

"I'm sorry about what happened on the trail." Jess said. "I promise it won't ever happen again. I don't know what overcame me." The silence became unbearable. "Are we still friends?" Her words sounded sincere.

I let another moment go by before I sighed and took a deep breath to get my voice to work. "Forget about it and I will too."

She patted my shoulder. "Thanks, Lora."

"Jess? What just happened? Did you see?"

"The deer ran from the forest. They were spooked or freaked out—"

Johnnie opened the driver's side door and flopped into the seat. He rubbed his face. "You need to go fill out a form thing with the cops. They want everyone's info."

37

Two pages and a billion questions later, Johnnie drove down the freeway. He didn't go faster than forty-five the entire way home. No one spoke until we arrived at Jess' house.

"You guys want to come in for a few?" Jess touched my shoulder.

"Yeah! That's a great idea." Johnnie turned the engine off and jumped out of the cab before I had a chance to respond.

"I'm real tired and want to go home for now," I said.

"Oh, okay. Do you want me to drive you?" Johnnie frowned.

"No, silly. I can walk."

"See you at work tomorrow then," Johnnie said without hesitation.

Jess' brows scrunched up. "Fine. I'll see you tomorrow night for the concert, around four."

I dragged myself up the hill to my house and replayed the accident over in my head. The figure in the forest must have been the big bear we saw in The Dalles. That's the only explanation I could think of.

My best friend all of a sudden wanted to make-out with me. This would never have happened before she left last June. She came back a completely different person.

I had lost my friend I knew. I didn't know this new version of my friend.

Weird things were happening and building on top of each other.

My insides ached.

The clouds lingered, trapping the thick air. Moisture grabbed onto my skin and clothes. Rain pinged and ponged onto the dry road.

I fell into bed, not even bothering to take anything off, and clutched my soft, cool pillow, closed my eyes and drifted away.

***

Dream Journal Entry: August 31^{*st*}

The fog floated all around me, clinging to me, blinding me. It seemed as though I had been walking in circles for hours trying to find my way out of the fog. The ground mushed under my heavy feet as I sludged my way through the mud and vegetation. The trees thickened. My breathing quickened at the thought that I may never find my way out.

I took a deep breath, allowing the cool air to fill my lungs. This calmed me. I searched for an end to the blinding forest.

The fog thinned directly in front of me and swirled around as if a wind blew it. But there was no wind.

A figure emerged from deep in the forest. As it approached, I recognized her. Her long, golden hair flowed behind her in soft curls. Her porcelain skin had a hint of flush in the cheeks. Her loving, light brown eyes filled with compassion, and her strawberry lips shimmered. An ivory chiffon dress hung from her shoulders, draped around her body and trailed through the mud at her feet.

Dream Mom.

I'd never seen a picture of my mom. I created that image of her in my head as a goddess with wind blowing through her hair and she never changed whenever I dreamt of her.

"Run, Lora." Her lips did not move but the words rang soft, without urgency, in my mind. Like a lullaby. "Run!" She said again in my mind but this time she raised her hand slowly and pointed behind me.

I didn't take my eyes off her beauty in fear she might disappear.

"Run, my love." Her eyes flashed stern, but her voice remained calm, almost serene.

My body turned toward where her hand pointed. I couldn't pull my eyes away from my mom, though. She nodded, so I turned my head. The fog lifted in that area. Trees and foliage stood rooted to the ground.

The ferns deep in the forest twitched. A large dark cloud with glowing blue eyes glaring at me appeared in the distance. The fog swirled around it.

A tingling sensation crept down the skin over my spine. Goosebumps rose over my entire body and my lungs felt heavy, making it hard to breathe. Horror sank deep into my gut. I froze while the creature transformed from fog to something dark and solid right before me.

Six

"Lora. Lora, honey, wake up!" Aubrey's voice boomed in my ear. "It's time to get up. You have work today, remember?"

I moaned, and then turned, throwing the blanket over my head. "I'm up." I rolled off the bed. Laundry and other clutter cushioned my landing. The clock read 9:15 AM.

"You must have been exhausted," Aubrey said. "You were asleep when I got home from work last night so I didn't wake you. Are you feeling alright?"

"Yeah. I don't know why I'm so tired lately."

Aubrey left my room, still talking. "I'm going to make some French toast. Do you want any?"

"Sure." My stomach groaned, which was weird because I didn't usually eat breakfast. I stumbled into the bathroom to take a quick shower and dress for work.

The bathroom filled with steam. I recalled the fog from my dream and a shiver dripped down my back. Wiping the mirror, my dream mother reflected back at me for just one second. I didn't look exactly like the mother in my dream, but I had many of the same features. My long golden hair, not as full and billowy as my mother's hair—and right then was very wet—resembled hers. My brown eyes and pale skin, not porcelain and beautiful, but pale nonetheless, also looked like hers. I loved the mother I created. She was beautiful.

I finished getting dressed in my black slacks and white shirt uniform, then walked into the kitchen. Aubrey sat at the center island on the bar stool, sipping a cup of coffee while reading the newspaper. A dirty plate lay in front of her and another plate of steaming French toast waited at the other bar stool. I shoveled the food into my mouth.

Aubrey dropped her newspaper to give me the look. "I don't want you hiking alone. There've been some weird animal attacks lately." She must have heard about the logger guy and then the accident. I never told her of the bear incident in The Dalles. She probably wouldn't let me out of her sight if she knew about that, too.

"'Kay." I gulped down a glass of milk in record time and didn't dare mention anything about my secret spot on the hill. If I went there with someone, it wouldn't be my secret spot anymore. I hadn't been up there since Saturday.

"I mean it." She didn't stop looking at me over her invisible glasses.

"Yeah. I get it. You got any more toast?"

"I made you four extra pieces. Did you eat them already?" Aubrey smirked, as if she knew something I didn't.

"You did? Huh. I guess so." Weird. I licked my plate clean.

Aubrey didn't work Tuesdays, so she curled up on the couch in her pajamas and read a book when I left for the diner. So not fair.

The sun burned at my eye level in the sky. The lack of clouds must have allowed all the warm air to spill away from yesterday because the morning had a chilly bite. The birds enjoyed the cool morning by bathing in the puddles along the road left over from yesterday's rain.

The diner sat only a few blocks down the hill. It hadn't changed much for as long as I could remember. When Johnnie's dad, Mr. Estes, bought it a couple years prior, he put in new carpet, tables, and chairs, but the layout stayed the same.

The windows in the front dining area kept it bright and cheery inside. The counter with swivel bar stools that the local regulars sat at had cracks and chips in the white tile top. Overall, the diner was pretty bland and nothing real special, but it did have a warm homey feel to it that I always liked. Being the only diner in town, I pretty much grew up in it. What it lacked in décor, it made up for in the famous yummylicious food and friendly service.

I made coffee behind the counter and was preparing the condiments for the day when Johnnie and his dad walked in. Mr. Estes stomped to his office in the back. Johnnie strolled to the counter.

"Hey, Lora. You look…tired." Johnnie grabbed a bundle of napkins to fill the dispensers with.

"Gee, thanks. What did you and Jess do yesterday after I left?"

"Nothing much," he mumbled. "She's really changed this summer, huh?"

"I'm glad I'm not the only one to notice."

"Yeah, she's not as fun no more. It's like she's got a million things to worry about now or something and hates everyone around her. Even her appearance is depressing. She used to be real cute." He paused for a moment before shrugging. "I didn't stay very long. All she wanted to do was mope on the couch and watch TV. I left after an hour when Mandy got home from work."

"Did she mention anything to you about what happened to Amy?" I asked.

"No, but my dad heard about it already. He told me last night after I got home. He was pretty relieved that we weren't hurt in that accident but said we shouldn't be out hiking alone." He rolled his eyes.

"Yeah, Aubrey was the same. Lame. I hope they figure out what's going on soon. It's kind of freaky."

"It'll suck not being able to ride my motorcycle in the woods for a while." Johnnie opened the front door for Steve and Rachael.

Steve, a small older man of Mexican descent, worked at the diner since before Mr. Estes bought it. Mr. Estes kept him on as the Kitchen Manager. Rachael worked there for the last year as a waitress. I liked Rachael more when she was at work because Dani wasn't around dictating her every move so she could have her own personality.

The lunch rush turned out to be a trickle. All my tables were empty near the end of my shift.

Johnnie told Rachael about what happened to us the day before. She was deeply enthralled in the story when the bell on the front door jingled. She didn't move to get it.

Whatever.

I glanced around the corner to gauge how many menus to grab. That's when I saw the supermodel water-bottle guy. The hottest guy ever. I jerked my head back so he couldn't see me. And then I peeked again.

He stood next to the counter with two other guys. Both of his friends wore dark sunglasses. He laughed and his head tilted back just right that his black silk hair shifted, like wind blew through it for a moment. His strong jaw clenched as if

44

sensing my stare and he turned so that his eyes locked with mine. I melted. I couldn't feel my body. It floated in midair, but not really. His vibrant clear blue eyes smiled at me.

Hello Lora. I heard his words as though he said them, but his lips did *not* move. I broke eye contact and I snapped my head back. I wasn't sure if I should be shocked that a stranger knew my name, weirded out that his lips didn't move, or embarrassed for peeking around the corner.

I took a deep breath and checked my reflection in the mirror on the wall behind me. I smoothed out my blond hair, patted the puffiness away around my brown eyes, and walked out front.

"Goof adernoon!" My voice trembled. OMG! "I mean, good afternoon. Uh. How many today?" Face. Really. Numb. Tongue totally swollen.

The two guys standing next to the hottest guy in the world laughed under their breaths.

My ears flared hot.

"Three, my sweet." His voice poured from his mouth smooth as hot fondue.

I froze with a fake gigantic smile on my face. It took every effort I could possibly find to get me to move and laugh my fake laugh (which sounded faker than ever, by the way).

He shifted his eyes to the menus and grinned for a second. He forced his breathtaking grin away, which he should never do in my humble opinion, and gazed right at me. Then he winked with an apologetic expression on his face.

I stepped forward to seat them in the closest booth as possible. I practically threw the menus on the table and

45

walked away so fast that I twisted my ankle. A twinge of pain surged up my leg. After a couple steps of limping, the pain faded and I zipped behind the wall of safety where Johnnie and Rachael stood yapping like nobody's business.

"Oh my gosh!" I had no breath as if I had just run around the block. "Rachael, you have to help me. There is no way I can serve this guy. Look! Look at *him*. Have you ever seen anything so beautiful?" I must have sounded pathetic because Rachael didn't move. She rolled her eyes instead.

"Don't be so dramatic," she said.

"Would you just look?"

Rachael poked her head around the corner and then faced me, biting her lip. A laugh burst from her mouth. Almost a hysterical laugh.

Anger washed over me. "What?"

She continued to laugh for a few seconds before composing herself. "Remember that guy that Dani is infatuated with?"

I nodded. Disappointment filled my chest.

"That's *him*!" She pointed toward the wall.

My mind blanked.

"Don't worry about it." Rachael let out a sigh. "I'll help them." She whisper-laughed and walked to the lobby to help the customers that I couldn't bear to look at again.

"Why don't you take off?" Johnnie smirked at me. I must have seemed like a little girl standing in front of a wall of candy. "You only have a few minutes left anyway. Aren't you going to the Bloody Pulp concert tonight with Jess?"

I bounced out of my trance at the opportunity to escape. "Okay." I didn't want to leave that gorgeous creature out front, but if I went out there again I might've fainted. I indulged in one more look around the corner.

The three of them sat while Rachael stood in front of their table taking orders. A half-grin appeared on water model's lips but he did not look at me. I memorized every feature of his face. From his strong jaw with the hint of a shadow, obvious that he hadn't shaven, to his etched cheek bones. His eyelashes were as black as his hair and super long, curling up just slightly.

Be well, Lora.

I jerked around to see if someone was behind me. No one. I must've been imagining things. I turned back.

He laughed.

I decided to slip out the back door before I went totally insane.

The air had warmed, but it was still cool enough to wake me from the weird spell *he* put on me. I strolled home, reliving the few minutes that had just passed in my mind. Now I understood why Dani was so infatuated. I wondered if I would ever see him again and if I did what I would say. Probably and probably something stupid.

I picked up my speed to get home, almost sure that I would see him again...almost.

Seven

Jess arrived on time.

I couldn't shake the image burned into my head. His face haunted my every thought—his penetrating eyes with his half-smile made me blush. Even far away from him, thinking about him gave me an uneasy feeling, like I should be afraid or jump his bones next time I see him. Two radically different scenarios, but both felt right.

Jess turned down the music about an hour into the drive. "So, uh, what's up with you?"

"Huh? What are you talking about?"

"Hello? You haven't said two words, since you got in the car. I thought we were cool."

"Oh, yeah. Sorry. Stomach's a bit queasy, I guess."

"You better not be getting sick. I've been looking forward to this concert all summer," she said.

"Nah, I'm fine. Just too excited, probably."

At the rate Jess drove, I thought it would take longer than the normal three hours to get to the Gorge Amphitheatre in George. She drove slower than any grandma I had ever seen. We arrived at and pulled into the dust-filled parking area. A dude with long limbs directed us to park near the exit of the field trampled by cars.

"I told you we should've left sooner." Jess had a sarcastic tone, but I knew she didn't intend to be funny.

After we waited in line, shuffled through the gate, had our bags searched, and our hands stamped to declare to the world our minor status, we arrived into vendor territory.

Vendors of all types pedaled their junk and food and beer under white canopies. The scent of fried food caused my mouth to water. Totally weird because I never liked fried food much, especially fried meat. Gross. But then, it didn't smell so gross, even though I had already had a Garden Burger on the way there.

We casually strolled past each booth. Occasionally, I found a pretty piece of handmade jewelry or some homemade soap that I stopped to look at, but couldn't afford to purchase. I spent most of my money already on half of the gas and parking and only had enough left for a soda.

It became difficult at times to squeeze through the massive crowd. I held the back of Jess' shirt with a death grip. We followed a heavily treed path, winding down the hill with a horde of other people. It soon led us to what normally would be a vast and empty area in front of the stage.

The setting sun scarred the sky with burns of deep purple and pink streaks behind the black iron stage. Below that, the land opened up for a reflection of the heavens that had etched its way through rocky earth and left jagged cliffs as a reminder to the world of water's force, even in the middle of desert lands.

Thousands of people crammed their way closer to the stage and filled the entire arena. The out-of-place grass was trampled flat and bald in some areas where people bounced to the rhythms.

We stood at the edge of the trees.

"There is no way we are getting near that stage!" I said over the music.

Jess grabbed my hand and darted toward the stage, ramming people out of our way while squeezing through any tiny gap to get closer.

Sandpaper brushed my lungs. Dead fish pits, ocean breath, road-kill ass, all invaded my nostrils. I could never be a sardine. I forced my arms out from my body, pushing random people away from me, to give me air.

Some band I had never heard of played on the stage. It hypnotized the audience to move in crazy gyrations, way too close to me. They hovered over and around me. Suffocating me.

We finally reached the fence about five feet from the stage. Jess had an accomplished look on her face when she said something that I couldn't understand.

A small droplet of moisture dripped from my forehead. "Great!" I threw my hands up gesturing to the sweat pouring down my face. Jess laughed her obnoxiously loud, evil laugh. I didn't think it was so funny considering I spent a good half an hour putting on mascara and black eye liner just for it to melt. I didn't usually wear makeup, but when I did, I wanted it to last.

People nudged even closer to me. Claustrophobia kicked in and I almost gagged, but calmed my breathing and imagined wide open spaces.

Finally, the band that I had never heard of finished their part of the concert. I looked over to Jess and our eyes met, filled with excitement for the concert we had waited forever to see.

The electricity in the air built around us and throughout the crowd.

Like a switch was thrown, the entire audience roared. I couldn't even hear my own screams. The lights flickered. Everyone twitched and jerked in the silver flashing light. Bloody Pulp rushed onto the stage, moving in a chopping fashion in the dance of strobe lights.

I grabbed Jess' shoulders from behind to shake her, in a teasing way, with anticipation. I couldn't stand the wait!

A beat of guitars and drums blasted through the crowd. The deafening scream of the audience could no longer be heard over the music. The vibrations rippled through my body.

Arms, legs, heads, chests all moved closer and closer. They compressed me against the fence, but I didn't budge my spot. I pushed my butt back, making some room and we jumped and danced. Everyone moved as one. We sang and yelled. My throat burned.

The drums kept rhythm and the guitars screeched along with the lyrics, controlling my body for nearly two hours.

I glanced over to find Jess, but she wasn't where I last saw her. I waited through one more song before turning to find only strangers' faces and sweaty bodies. She wouldn't have gone far without telling me.

I moved away from the fence and pushed and squeezed through the tight crowd. The further from the stage I got, the looser the bodies became.

Back at the forest, small groups of people partied in the dark of the night. One couple made out on a picnic bench, others drank beer and smoked cigarettes. The music echoed off the trees, whispers blew in the warm summer breeze, and Jess wasn't to be found.

Maybe she hadn't left the stage after all. A bazillion people crawled and hopped like a colony of ants. Flashes of color illuminated arms and heads in split seconds of time. If she was still down there, I wouldn't find her.

I staggered from one foot to the other to ease the ache from standing all day at work and then the concert.

A giant rip in my rocker t-shirt, that I didn't notice before, exposed my belly. Great. We were crammed so tight at times against the chain link fence, it probably snagged on a sharp edge. The dim light pointed out the obvious sweat stains from my pits. Double great. I bet my makeup and hair were just as disgusting.

I paced in front of the trees. The single light that hovered nearby went black. The glow from the stage didn't reach that far. "It just figures!" I whispered to the universe.

An awareness pricked my senses that someone was watching me. I zipped around but only dark trees stood behind me and haze from two guys smoking at the picnic table several yards away. They spoke to each other, but they didn't seem to notice me.

I shrugged it off and allowed the music to move me again. Closing my eyes and using the tree for support, I swayed to the rhythm. The summer air filled my lungs: warm grass, pine, and sap with traces of stale fried food, garbage, and lingering cigarette smoke. My mind felt heavy, the music pounded in my ears, as though I still stood only feet away from the speakers.

A new song began. A familiar scent mixed in with the others. I opened my eyes. Straight ahead of me, coming out of the darkness, his warm clear eyes penetrated through me. His muscular build sent my pulse racing.

When he stepped from the trail, a random light from the stage flashed against his moist, golden tanned chest. My breathing pretty much stopped.

A half-buttoned white shirt clung to his body. He stepped with determination straight toward me. With a half-grin on his lips, he never once took his eyes from mine. My legs turned into earthworms and flutters made their way into my stomach.

How was it possible to see him twice in the same day at two radically different locations?

Everything slowed, his determined walk, the slight breeze through his dark hair. The few people strolling around me turned to blurred smudges of color. It took him forever before he reached and stopped inches from me—finally. The earth-like musk scent sweltering off his body stirred my blood and I felt a little woozy.

His hands motioned to touch my face, yet, they didn't touch me. He held them close to my skin, enveloping my cheeks. Heat emanated off his body and wrapped around mine. He still didn't touch me. I felt and smelled his tantalizing breath. Fire filled my every cell. Please, just touch me.

Electricity pulsated from his hands and created shock waves through my head. I tried to grab them, but he moved away. His eyes, still locked with mine, laughed. His smile grew wide and exposed white teeth. *Am I really admiring his teeth right now?*

My pulse sped faster and my body wouldn't stop moving to the rhythm of the music. His body moved symmetrically with mine, without touching for the duration of the song.

Just touch me!

The song ended. We stopped.

"Lora," a faraway voice called from behind me.

I tore my eyes away from his to find the source. No one. I turned back.

He was gone.

I searched from left to right.

"Lora." The desperation in the call made me cringe. Jess stomped toward me with a clenched jaw and forced-together brows. She looked insane. I should've run away. "Where were you? I've been totally freaking out!"

I reorganized the thoughts in my muddled head. "Uh, I've been here. Where have *you* been? One minute you were next to me and the next, you were gone."

"I didn't go anywhere, *Lora!*" She pointed to the stage. "I was down there the entire time you were, and then I saw *you* leave. I followed you, but lost you in the crowd." The irritation in her voice slipped away. Her face turned from red to a soft shade of pink.

"Seriously? I didn't see you and panicked, so I went to look for you." I tried to shrug off her anger. "Sorry. You know how I get in a large crowd. I couldn't see you and I needed air."

"So, who was that guy you were talking to?" Ice ripped through her voice.

"I'm not sure." I searched the trees again. "Did you see where he went?"

She rolled her eyes. "No."

54

The concert ended. The crowd cheered for an encore. We walked toward the gate. I turned to look for him one more time. Nothing.

My heart dropped to my feet and an ache clogged my abdomen. Emptiness filled my being. We drove the long journey home in silence.

Eight

Labor Day. Almost an entire week after the concert with no word from Jess. One more day of freedom before school started, and no sign of the super-hot water bottle model either. His scent lingered with me and not a day went by that week I didn't dream about him.

With my arms full of beach towel, sun screen, journal, giant wicker hat, and sunglasses, I trekked through the sweltering parking lot of Doug's Beach. The heat rose from the asphalt, melting my flip-flops. If he was anywhere around, he'd be at Doug's Beach, known as a world premier windsurfing area.

My enthusiasm dampened with the sight of only two vehicles in the parking lot. It was still early though, so I waited on the rocky beach.

People trickled into the park. Kids played, seagulls screamed, wind whistled, the river lapped, and my eyes grew heavy. I shook the sleep away and focused on my journal. I had nothing to write. No words formed.

In the distance, sails jerked up and down on the choppy waves. One in particular, an aqua green color, spent more time in the air than on the water.

The sun felt good. I stretched and turned on my side, bending my knees just enough to be in a loose fetal position and watched the bobbing sails. My eyes grew dry and I closed them for a moment to wash the sting away.

The concert seemed like forever ago, he seemed like a dream. I relived every detail in my mind from the enticing scent of his warm skin to the white sparkle of his teeth to the soft texture of his wavy black hair.

***

Dream Journal Entry: September 6

Fog surrounded me with blinding thickness. The ground was sand and not mushy and wet. The air was warmer and not as moist. Waves lapped on a shore in the distance.

Wandering through fog, I followed the sound of the waves with my hands outstretched so I wouldn't run into a cliff or rock. I walked forever, never reaching the water.

The fog thinned in front of me and swirled around. A broad-shouldered figure approached.

My breath caught in my throat. He shook his head and droplets of water flew from his wet black hair, not yet close enough to reach me.

He moved in slow motion. My heart sped faster the closer he got. The features on his face became visible. His soft skin smoothed over a strongly pronounced jaw, nose, and cheek bones. He'd shaved since the last time I saw him. His eyes, the brilliant blue that somehow seemed warm, were crystal clear, like ice, locked with mine. A half-grin turned up on one side of his face.

His earthy musk scent stirred every fluid in my body, flushing my head with blood, giving me a heavy-headed sensation.

"My sweet." His lips did not move. For some reason this didn't seem odd to me. His hands moved to hold my face, but they froze in midair, never reaching me.

His eyes changed from warm and caring into something indescribably frightening. His head snapped to the left.

A deep growl came from the direction he looked, its source hidden by the fog.

The muscles in his arms and chest pulsated and grew right before me. He met my eyes once again. "Run, my sweet!" His words rang in my mind.

My body did not move but I wanted to obey him—his caring words echoed through my mind. His head jerked to the left again and he threw himself down on all fours. He wasn't himself, but something—not someone—else.

The growling increased, deep and dark.

He ran into the fog toward the growl.

He disappeared. The growling stopped.

***

My eyes opened, as if cued by an outside force that my dream had ended and it was time to wake up. A person sat next to me on my towel. I yawned and stretched, still dreaming. A gull flew above in the powder blue sky. Children played in the distance.

A man near me coughed. I turned my head and then jolted to a seated position. Super-hot model dude sat right next to me on my very own beach towel. For real, not a dream. He looked down at me. I forgot to breathe again.

"Good morning, my sweet." He winked. "I hope you don't mind that I waited for you to wake." His lower lip pouted. I bit mine.

Nothing came from my mouth. His hand brushed my cheek, actually touching me. Goosebumps took over my face.

"You were so peaceful. I'm sorry if I woke you, Lora." His eyes twinkled.

"How do you know my name?" I shocked myself with real words.

He shrugged. "I asked around."

"You asked around about *me*? Why would you do that?"

He winked again. My body softened into putty sitting on the towel. "I'm Chance Miller. It's wonderful to finally meet you."

Again, no words. Nothing. Silence. I stared at him leaning over me. The sunlight draped its warm rays around his head making him look as serene as an angel. I tried to wrap my head around his beauty and to accept the fact that my previous experiences with Chance were not hallucinations but real, unless of course, I was still dreaming. That would explain things much better than I was able to at that moment.

"I've seen you in town a few times this summer and asked around a bit just to find out who you were. I'm not a stalker or anything like that." He hinted at a small laugh.

"Oh, you're not? How come you just didn't ask me?" More understandable words. Amazing.

A musical sound came from his lips. His eyes lit up and his head flung back. I must've been in a soap opera. His laugh. OMG. "How could I have approached such a beautiful girl? I had no idea what to say."

My turn to laugh. "Yeah, umm, okay. I like that answer. So, to officially introduce myself," I extended my hand to shake his, "my name is Lora Jones."

He grasped my hand and pulled it toward his face. His breath warmed the skin on my hand when he held it up to his lips and kissed the backside without breaking eye contact with me. "It is a blessing to finally meet you my sweet Lora. May I take you to lunch?" His touch sent chills up my arm.

I nodded.

"Great!" He jumped up and extended a hand to assist me. He gathered his gear, grabbed my towel, and wrapped everything up under one arm faster than I could blink, let alone comprehend what I'd just agreed to. He gestured for me to follow him and walked backward, not taking his eyes off of me.

He led the way up the beach toward the trail to the parking lot. Eyes burned the back of my head, watching me, judging me. I turned around. People lounged on beach chairs or on blankets. They had picnics and played in the sand and some even swam and splashed in the water. I hadn't noticed that many people before then.

Dani Towner sat in a low profile beach chair at the other end of the beach. She wore a hot pink bikini top and matching sarong wrapped around her waist. Her stare did not move nor hesitate. Quickly, I turned away, pretending not to see her.

I remembered then that Dani came to the beach to watch a windsurfer with clear blue eyes. At the diner Rachael had said he was the guy Dani liked. I took a step forward, then glanced back one more time. Her eyes didn't budge.

Pushing the guilt away, I turned away from Dani and followed *my* windsurfer to the trail. He walked backward, watching me and then flashed his half-smile.

The thought of Dani left my mind.

Nine

Chance strapped his surfboard to the top of a shiny newer black Jeep pimped out with tinted windows and all the whistles, including fancy chrome wheels.

He held the passenger side door open for me. My car sat lonely in the corner of the lot.

"We'll be back, Lora." He answered my hesitation.

I skipped the remaining few feet and jumped into the front seat of his Jeep. The hot air inside smelled of Chance's earthy aroma mixed with new car scent and leather. He hopped into the driver's seat. "What would you like to eat today?"

I couldn't wipe the stupid grin off my face. "Wherever you go, I'll find something to eat. You choose the place."

"When do I need to get you home by?"

My face flushed warm. I hadn't thought of being out late in a long time and Aubrey had never set a curfew for me. It never came up in the past. Lunch couldn't be that far, but he must have had dinner plans too, or something. Aubrey would be home that evening from her weekend trip to Portland and school started the next day. She probably wouldn't appreciate it if I was out very late. "Nine, I guess."

"That gives us several possibilities. Although I would love to kidnap you and keep you forever, we will have to do with the nine hours you have graced me with. We won't go too far then." He pulled out of the parking lot, his jeep tires squealed and then we took off down the highway.

Unease pickled my guts. The tinted windows made the inside of the car darker than I was used to, like we were stuffed into a box and no one from the outside world could see us. "What do you mean kidnap?" I squirmed in the black leather seat and a nervous laugh escaped from my mouth. "We are just going to lunch, right? Or, uh, what do you have planned? A trip around the world?"

Chance laughed his supermodel way where his dark hair tumbled backward and his tan skin stretched across his face, exposing gleaming white teeth. "Don't worry. I'm just teasing you. We aren't going very far."

"Whew." I exhaled. His words washed all threat away. "I kind of made it easy for you if you were an ax murderer rapist dude instead of a super hot dude..." I bit my lip and then my tongue. I'm an official dork.

"If I were an ax murderer rapist, yes, you are an easy victim." He winked. "Tell me, Lora, how has life treated you thus far?"

I giggled and then wanted to slap myself. "Uh, fine, I guess." Weird. "What do you mean?" Sweat trickled down the back of my neck.

He reached to the electric-blue buttons and knobs on the dash and pushed a few of them. Cold air whooshed out of the vents on both sides of the dash.

"Well, my sweet, life is about to get much better. We might have a few rough spots coming up, but things will always get better." He stated matter-of-factly and glanced at me with a twinkle in his eye.

"My life's been fine and it's just beginning, I have many more years to come. Is that what you mean?" He must have needed to ask weird questions to reduce his cuteness factor or something.

"Exactly! Your life is just beginning, Lora. This is so very true. Probably more true than you realize."

Umm, okay, or maybe he was a little bit crazy. Not everyone can be beautiful and sane all at the same time.

We didn't go very far at all, just like he promised. We stopped at the nearest town, Lyle. He parked the Jeep on Main Street in front of an old brick building that sold antiques.

Stepping down from the Jeep, I tripped. He caught me by reaching over from the driver's seat and grabbing my arm. His grip sent pulses of electricity from my elbow to my chest. He didn't even flinch at my weight, the strength of his one arm held me in place until I found my balance.

"Oops!" I giggled in embarrassment and bit my lip again to stop the insane sound. "Thanks." Shoot. Me. Now. Or just staple my mouth shut.

"Anytime and every time, my sweet."

His little nickname for me made me cringe. Although it was very flattering and all that he spent so much attention on me, his arrogance and pet name 'my sweet' started to eat my insides—just a little.

He took a few steps forward. I bolted to catch up and then walked next to him, sometimes skipping a step or two to keep up.

Old brick buildings, weathered from time, held "Closed" signs in their dirty storefront windows. Crab grass clung to cracks in the sidewalk, and I made sure not to step on any of them so I wouldn't break my mother's back. The sound of the river lapping at the near shore was occasionally washed out by a car zipping by on the highway.

I pulled my floppy straw hat from my bag and put it on for shade from the sweltering sun and wiped the sweat from my brow.

Lyle's the type of town that people, including me, drive through on their way to somewhere else. We were walking through one of those pictures that hang in museums to show what life used to look like a long time ago, but our picture was in color.

We passed a hardware store and a little grocery market with an "Open" sign buzzing in the window and several homes that were probably considered historical with white picket fences, blooming rose gardens and well maintained green grass, despite the sweltering summer we'd had.

Chance slowed his stride.

"Are you going to tell me where you're kidnapping me to?" The irritation in my voice startled me, so I giggled to cover it up, which made it worse.

With that, he touched my hand ever so lightly and looked directly into my eyes. His face, only inches from mine, and his warm breath tickling my nose, he said, "You'll see." He brushed my cheek with his hand. "Shall we continue?"

This time when we walked, he didn't let go of my hand. It felt strange to walk with a complete stranger in a foreign town so close to home, yet I felt comfortable and safe as if I'd known him forever, for my entire life. I must have been going crazy. Of the very few guys that I dated in the past, there were never any sparks like with Chance. I always

64

thought people made that stuff up just to make life seem more interesting than it really was.

Chance pulled me down an alley with trash cans lining the back of buildings.

The river rushed ahead and once we got to the end of the street, we turned onto a broken cobblestone boardwalk that followed the mighty Columbia River. The cobblestones must have been there for years and years because they had cracks and broken edges that crumbled to gravel when we stepped on them.

The wind off the river dried up all the sweat that lingered on my skin. It blew through my skirt and through my hair, cool and wonderful.

We followed the boardwalk for several minutes and then stopped at a building from an ancient era. I kinked my head up at the narrow, tall cottage painted white with a gray trim. Large windows on each of the three levels faced the river. A balcony on the top floor held a small iron table and colorful flowers in little baskets hanging from the railing.

Chance pushed open the weathered front door inlaid with panes of stained glass. The hinges cried in protest.

A black iron staircase twisted upward, not stopping until the very top floor. Mildew and a mixture of rosemary, thyme, and the earthy musky scent that lingered on Chance rose from the interior. Dark hardwood floors bled into the walls and up to the halfway point where the wall turned into an art gallery with a red backdrop. Sunlight shined through the stained glass in the front door and cast colorful lights on the dark floors. Yellow roses wilted in a crystal vase next to the staircase.

"Welcome to my home. This is where I live when I'm here for windsurfing." He grasped both of my hands and looked at me. "I hope you feel comfortable here."

I wanted to gush to him how awesome his pad was and how it felt so warm and cozy and that I couldn't wait to see the rest of it, but my tongue got tied to my tonsils.

The wind whistled down the stairs, sounding like music. I laughed and twirled around as if dancing, and for once didn't give a care about how silly it seemed.

Chance's shoulders relaxed and he beamed. "Mrs. Olsen!" he yelled.

I froze.

"Yes, Mr. Miller," a small voice echoed down the stairs and a stout round lady peeked over the second floor railing.

"I have a guest. This is Lora and she'll be having lunch with me today."

"Wonderful! Would you like to be served on the balcony?"

"That would be great, Mrs. Olsen." Chance winked at me, grabbed my hand and led me up the stairs to the third floor.

To the left of the staircase stood a giant four-poster bed with white chiffon draped over the canopy and a white down comforter covering the thick mattresses and white velvet throw pillows piled high at the head. French doors opened to the balcony, allowing the cool breeze to billow through white curtains hanging from the doors.

I stepped onto a fluffy white carpet that clung to the dark wood floors at the foot of the bed and traced my hand over a velvet white couch.

The butter cream walls added a cheery contrast to the crispness of everything else and the crystal chandelier hanging above the staircase reflected rainbows dancing along the walls.

I walked over to a cobblestone fireplace with a pile of chopped wood sleeping inside, waiting to ignite. No pictures lay on the mantel, no loved ones graced any of the walls of the cottage.

Chance appeared next to me and led me to the balcony. The sunlight reflected off the water and giant mountains hovered over the river, making us appear as ants in the ancient Gorge.

He pulled a chair over that shouldn't have been outside and gestured for me to sit. Velvety fabric covered soft cushions that held the heat from the sun. Chance sat in a similar chair in front of me on the other side of the small glass and iron table.

As if on cue, Mrs. Olsen stepped onto the balcony with two salads on small glass plates in her hands. Her face told her life with wrinkles around her eyes and laugh lines around her mouth. Salt and pepper hair was neatly pulled into a twist on the back of her head. She placed the salads on the table.

"Thank you," I said.

"You're very welcome." She nodded. Chance gave her a wink and she disappeared back the way she came.

I waited to pick up my fork, unsure and a bit self conscious about eating in front of him. I forgot about my anxiety when he began chowing down on his salad as if he had never eaten before.

To my astonishment he finished his salad before I took one bite. He must have felt me staring at him because he stopped just before he shoved the last piece of lettuce in his mouth and grinned at me. "Eat!"

I stabbed a fork full of lettuce and analyzed the oily dressing before stuffing it into my mouth. Amazing salad dressing! Forgetting about Chance staring at me, I too shoveled lettuce into my mouth like a gold digger. Chance chuckled softly.

"What kind of dressing is this?" I asked between swallows.

He shrugged. "It's one of those secret recipes that old people like to keep to themselves. Mrs. Olsen makes the best of everything."

Again, on cue, Mrs. Olsen walked out carrying two plates piled high with steaming food. I'm not sure exactly what it was but it looked like some kind of cow. It was so red and bloody, it seemed raw, but it must have been cooked because it was hot. Little red potatoes and bright green beans sat next to the pile of bloody flesh.

"I hope you enjoy your meat rare." Mrs. Olsen held a question in her expression.

"Actually," I swallowed, hard, not wanting to hurt her feelings. "It's, uh, fine."

"I assure you, you'll enjoy it." Mrs. Olsen responded with confidence and a little nod of agreement to her own statement. To tell the truth, I hadn't eaten meat for years. The whole concept of dead flesh in my mouth always made me gag out of disgust and then cry for the poor creature who had suffered death so I could digest it.

Chance chowed down again, pausing for air a few times. I picked at the dead cow or whatever it was with zero intention of eating the bloody mess. Maybe if I moved it around on the plate, it wouldn't be as rude. The metallic smell made my mouth water, though, going against everything I knew. I sawed off a small piece and raised it to my lips. I filled my lungs with breath and pushed the fork into my mouth.

OMG. Flavor, satisfying every bud on my tongue, burst from the meat. I shoved another bite into my mouth, enjoying the salty taste and stringy texture of muscle fibers between my teeth, which should have made me vomit, but didn't. What had I been missing for so many years? Before I knew it, the piece of carcass was gone. And with it, not a single drop of guilt lingered. What was *wrong* with me?

"You are *so* lucky to be able to eat like this every day!" I said with more excitement in my voice than I intended.

"I'll have to agree with you there. Mrs. Olsen is the best at everything, actually. She even windsurfs!" Chance stated that last part with sarcasm and then with a more serious tone, "She's perfect."

I licked my plate clean and sat back in the soft chair and closed my eyes. I tried to remember how perfect the scene was on the other side of my eyelids. Chance sat at the table with his cheek resting on one hand, gazing. Behind him, golden sunlight sparkled on top of the deep blue river. The sky played backdrop to the dark silhouette of mountains.

That moment was burned into my mind, forever, I hoped. I opened my eyes and met Chance's calm and gentle gaze.

"Tell me about yourself, Lora."

"What do you want to know?"

"Everything that there is to know." Chance sat back in his chair.

"Well, I was born in White Salmon at the hospital on the hill. My mother's name was Sabrina—"

"Was?"

"Are you going to let me tell my story?" I asked.

"Oh, yes. Sorry. Please continue." He held out his hand, gesturing for me to continue, all formal-like.

"Uh, 'kay. I don't know my father. His name isn't on my birth certificate. I've lived in the same house forever with my godmother, Aubrey. My mom lived there, too, before she disappeared. One morning, when I was one, she just never came home. The police searched for her for weeks. They found her car parked in an alley in Portland a few days later. No trace of her was ever found and Aubrey has been taking care of me ever since then." I refilled my lungs. "That's my lame life in thirty seconds. As soon as I graduate high school, I'm moving far away from small towns."

"Where will you go?" He said the question more like a statement, as if he already knew the answer.

"To start, me and my best friend, Jess, have been planning to move to Seattle for school. After that, who knows?" I shrugged. "Maybe I'll travel the world or something."

"I'd love to travel the world with you." Chance flashed his half-grin and rested one leg over the opposite knee.

"Oh, really?" My voice shook on a nervous knot. I cleared it from my throat. "Is that how this plays out? You're going to kidnap me and take me around the world?" That might have been cool, though. Kidnapped by a gorgeous surfer to travel around the world with him— a tragic nightmare. "It's your turn to tell me about you. What's your story?"

"I don't really have one. Mrs. Olsen has always been here for me to take care of my needs. My parents, who are never around, have enough money to live on for several lifetimes so I travel and enjoy what life has to offer on their tab." He crossed his arms in front of his chest, seeming proud of the small glimpse into his life. "Tell me more about you."

"That's not fair!"

"You'll see soon enough that it is, my sweet." His smooth, deep voice threw a calm trance over me, like a lullaby has on a child, not that I needed calming.

"Okay," I said. He reached across the table and held my hand.

"So, uh...um. What were we talking about?" I laughed. My clammy hand tingled under the warmth of his. "Oh yeah, so, uh, what else do you want to know?"

"Let's start with how old you are."

"I'll turn eighteen on November 26th." I paused. Eighteen had always seemed so far away, and now it was almost here. "How old are you?"

"We're talking about you now. Me later." He stood and led us inside the house to the white velvet couch. He wrapped one arm around me. My body melted next to his warm-soft-hard chest and my head fell onto his shoulder. He stroked my hair, sending electric currents through each root into my scalp. It hit me. Extremely hot water bottle model, who happened to simultaneously be a stranger, was stroking my hair! It was like one of those stranger danger commercials, except I didn't feel in danger. In fact, if I were a cat, I would have purred. It felt right lying next to him. Chance. My Chance. I closed my eyes for a moment.

71

When I opened them, after what seemed like a minute, the golden light shining in through the doors had turned into an indigo glow. It took a few moments for this to register but once it did, I jolted up and looked around the dark room.

"It's okay, my sweet." The chocolaty voice came from outside and then he appeared in a chair near the doors, watching me. His eyes blazed against dark skin. He smiled, almost blinding me with white teeth.

"What time is it?" I cleared my throat.

"It's only a little after eight. We still have time to get you back by nine."

"I'm so sorry. I don't know how I could have fallen asleep." I had the opportunity of a lifetime to spend an entire afternoon with him and I fell asleep. Lame.

"Don't worry. We'll see each other again. Besides, you're pretty cute when you sleep."

I held the giggle from escaping my lips.

"Answer a question for me before we leave, though," he said.

"Okay." I twisted my legs into a pretzel and pulled my blond hair off my shoulders. He moved from the chair and sat next to me, holding my hand again. "Have you always had that mark on the back of your arm?" He brushed the skin covering my left tricep with his fingertips.

"My birthmark? Yeah, it's kind of ugly, but luckily it's so small that I don't even notice it. Is it that noticeable?"

"Not at all and I think it's beautiful." Confusion blotted his eyes. He pulled away and stared out the doors for a moment, then snapped out of his trance. He wrapped both of his hands onto my face and brushed my cheeks, and then rested them on my shoulders. "Lora, I know we've just met and you may think this is all very strange, but you're very special to me. You don't know much about me, but I know you see what I'm talking about. I know you feel the magic between us." His face moved close to mine—his lips brushed my cheek.

I must have stopped breathing. All the blood in my body poured into my face. Finally, a surge of cool air from the river filled my lungs. It smelled of sun dried moss and grass, and it mingled with Chance's scent. My eyes opened to see his beautiful face smiling at me again. He pulled me up and we went down the stairs and out the front door.

Red and purple and blue streaked the sky above the river—my favorite time of day in the summer. The air felt somewhat cooler than evenings in the past. We took our time on the cobblestone path. He held my hand, not once letting go. The water teased the stone littered beach with brief caresses, as if it was a sin for them to touch for too long. Caress and release, caress and release. I wondered what he thought about, why his forehead held a crinkle of concern and his jaw clenched periodically. But then he looked at me and the wondering disappeared with his worries.

Not a single word broke the silence until Chance pulled his Jeep into the parking lot of Doug's Beach. My car sat alone in the dark corner, waiting for my return.

Chance walked around the Jeep to open the door for me. Some crazy urge caused me to wrap my arms around him. His body went stiff and I pulled away, but he laughed and lifted me off the ground. We twirled round and round, my feet flew out from beneath me and my body swung like a helicopter blade. When we stopped, his lips released soft panting breaths, and my hand, without consulting me, touched his cheek. My suspicions were correct—the soft skin on his face felt warm and smooth. He closed his eyes, leaned into my neck and took a deep breath, as if I had scratch and sniff hair. He held me close for several moments and then let go.

"Goodnight my beautiful Lora."

"Goodnight my handsome prince." I bit my lip and wished to the gods of words to take mine back. I did not just call him that. Ugh.

He didn't seem to notice, or maybe the gods heard me. He said, "I'll see you tomorrow after school."

Back to reality. I sighed, not looking forward to school and only wanting to stay with Chance.

He followed me out of the parking lot all the way to Lyle. My heart stopped when he exited the highway.

The stars continued to twinkle in the black sky. The world did not end. I drove home.

Alone. Again.

Ten

Dream Journal Entry: September 7th

His scent permeated the diluted fog. It hovered over the ground, drawing a line through the forest. Particles of musky-earth moisture clung to my hair and clothes and skin. I crouched below the fog line near the moss covered ground, surrounded by him, and breathed him into my lungs. He filled and saturated every cell of my body. "My sweet Lora." His voice echoed in my mind. "You know what this means, don't you?"

"No," I said with my thoughts. "What does it mean, my prince?"

Deep from within the forest, a growl rumbled toward me. The ground trembled as if the forest did the growling. I jolted up to a standing position and looked aimlessly around from left to the right and found only trees filtering golden rays of sunlight. The growl grew louder. I ducked below the fog line again, feeling safer with him around me, his cloak protecting me from whatever may be here to harm me.

"The mark on your arm," the fog said to me. "It's what I've been searching for."

"Run," my dream-mom's voice said. She appeared next to me, sitting on a boulder covered with green-life. A large bullfrog sat at her feet. His chest stretched, like bubble gum, heaving in and out. It called out, reminding me of a child scraping her teeth on a balloon. R-uun, r-uun, r-uun...

The fog thinned. "No, please don't go!" I pleaded with Chance-fog, but it was too late. He was gone. Dream-mom vanished, too. The frog remained, but stopped his ranting. He sat silent at the base of the rock and snapped his tongue into the air, catching an invisible bug.

I hid my face in my arms and no longer cared about the stupid growling. Without Chance, the growling could eat me up and poop me out for all I cared.

The earth pounded beneath me. One pound. Two pounds. Three pounds. Silence.

My body stiffened. Hot rotten breath hit the back of my neck. My breathing quickened. Time slipped by. Finally, I could no longer take the heavy air on my shoulders and lifted my head to take a peek. Brown fur held droplets of moisture. I cranked my neck back. Two blue eyes pierced through the mass of fur, a wet black nose flared with breath, and giant gray teeth protruded from the mouth of the brown bear hovering over me. It stood up on its hind legs and opened its enormous mouth to let out a roar that should have burst my ear drums.

Uncontrollable tears burned down my face. Caring returned. I no longer wanted to be eaten and pooped out. I scurried away, pushing with my feet against the slippery forest floor and sliding my butt as far away as I could before hitting a tree about four feet away.

The bear stepped within inches of my face, opened his mouth once more to expose his dagger teeth and roared. Drool and spit speckled onto my skin and I gagged, pushing down stomach acids churned up from the aroma of rotten flesh.

Instead of vomiting last night's dinner, I let out a growl that equaled the bear's. The bear froze, still just inches away, probably just as startled at the noise that just burst from me as I was. Our eyes locked.

The bushes on the left rustled. We broke our stare-down.

Chance leaned against a tree with his arms across his chest. He smiled and winked, all supermodel like. I sighed.

The bear roared, snapping me out of la-la land.

"This is no time for posing, my prince," I thought to him.

The bear lunged for Chance.

They disappeared into the forest.

***

I shot out of bed, looking around my room in a daze of confusion. The back of my neck was wet with sweat—my hair and pillow were drenched. A soft gray light seeped into my room from the edge of the curtains. Morning had come.

The alarm clock on the nightstand beeped to interrupt my nightmares, which lingered like the smoke long after a fire had been extinguished. My eyes burned from the fight to keep them open. Waking never hurt that bad before. If only I could have lay there for five more minutes, nestled next to the warm, soft blanket, I would have been in heaven. Morning sucked.

I kicked the covers off and crept out of bed. My joints popped like an old lady's and my muscles ached. The bed called me back, but I fought the urge to return and stepped in the shower and then dressed for school. I didn't really feel like putting on make-up or doing my hair, so I decided to deal with a naked face and enjoyed the extra ten minutes in the cozy recliner.

The face of the grandfather clock against the wall stared at me. Tick. The short hand pointed to the seven and the long hand pointed to the four, giving the appearance that Mr. Grandfather Clock had grown a mustache since the last time I saw him. Tock. Tick. Tock.

The thought of Chance felt unreal, like an imaginary boyfriend. The events of the day prior were just wishful thinking. Tick. A hallucination. He was, after all, the hottest guy on the face of the freaking planet. Tock. After a while with him, it began to feel almost natural to be next to such a rare person. It felt awesome when he touched me and the sound of his voice echoed in my mind. Tick. My stomach ached from being away from him. We should never be apart. I had to see him. If only the day would be over and I could drive out to his place, just to be sure he was real. Tock. The ache grew more intense the more I thought about it.

The phone screamed. I jolted from out of the warm chair to answer it.

"So, you picking me up or what?" Jess' voice snapped in my ear.

We hadn't planned on anything which was weird because we always went to school together. We used to walk there before we got our licenses and last year we took turns driving even though school was only about a mile from our houses. Any excuse to sleep just a tiny bit longer was a good excuse.

"Be right there." I hung up the phone, stuffed an apple and a granola bar into my backpack and headed out the door. A layer of fog covered the world. I froze and then pinched myself to make sure I wasn't dreaming again. Ouch. The cool air clung to the car and windshield and my bare arms. I ran back into the house to grab a sweater. I locked the front door, turned, and saw the best thing to get rid of the gloomy day.

Chance stood across the street, leaning against his black Jeep with his hands stuffed into his jeans. If I were a photographer, this would be the shot I'd choose for the cover of Hot Guy Magazine. He stared at me. I ran across the street as fast as I could, remembering not to flail my arms into the air like a little girl who just got a pony for Christmas.

His arms spread open to catch me and I ran right into them. They enveloped me, holding me close, all warm and cozy.

Good morning, my sweet. His voice, like velvet, echoed in my mind. It didn't come from his body because I would have felt the vibrations on his chest, which I clearly did not. Looking up at his face, I searched his eyes to make sure I wasn't hallucinating again.

"Did you just say something?" I asked.

"I only wished you a good morning. Are you feeling alright? You look very tired."

"I'm so much better now." I buried my face in his strong chest. A hushed laugh rumbled against my cheek. "Say something else," I said.

"What would you like for me to say?"

I stopped myself mid-giggle. "Nothing. That'll do. I just wanted to hear your voice in your chest. Sometimes I think I'm hearing things that really aren't being said. It's like I can read your mind or something."

"Is that a bad thing? Maybe we are connected and you know what I want to say before I say it."

My eyes bulged. Maybe.

He laughed. Probably at me. "Would you mind if I come see you after school today?"

"I'll mind if you don't! I don't know how I'm going to get through today, but at least I'll have something to look forward to if you come back."

"It's a date, my sweet." He kissed me on the head and touched my cheek with his hand. It felt wrong to pull away.

"This afternoon, then." He winked.

"Okay." I couldn't force the smile off my face.

He hopped into his Jeep and drove down the road, turning at the end toward the main drive.

I took a breath, then let out a deep sigh. His Jeep disappeared around the corner and took my heart with it.

When I opened my car door, a single red rose sat on my seat.

***

Jess waited on the bench in front of her house. She took her time trampling through the wet grass to reach the car. "Hey." She greeted me with a fake-grin that vanished when she got in. "I can't believe we have to go back already. This bites."

"Right?" My tongue almost burst at the seams. I'd never kept a secret from Jess before, especially one about potential boyfriends. She'd been acting so weird, one minute she had attitude, the next she tried to kiss me, and then another she flipped back to normal. So, I kept Chance from her. At least until she normalled-out for a longer space of time. "Only one more year, though. So that's cool," I said.

"Yeah." She gazed out the window the entire three-minute drive to school.

We hadn't been assigned our senior parking spot yet, so we parked up front. Just when I turned off the car, Dani and Rachael strode past us in their new back-to-school outfits. Not that back-to-school clothes looked any different than anything else they ever wore, they just seemed to look shinier today for some reason. Rachael waved. Dani turned to face the other way, as if she didn't see us.

I grimaced, and dread gurgled in my stomach.

"Jess, before we go into the school there is something you should probably know."

She closed the door she had already opened. "What's up?"

"So, I met this guy, which is no big deal, but it may have gotten me in trouble with, uh, Dani."

"Really? Who is it? What do you mean by trouble?" Jess' face lit up.

I told her the story from when I first saw Chance up until that morning. I left out most of the details though. I had to tell her about him. No doubt, Dani would have spread the rumors across the school by lunch time. If Jess found out that I kept that kind of secret from her, she'd never speak to me again.

"Sweet. I wish I'd been at the beach just to see Dani's face." Jess laughed. "Priceless." She nodded her head and stepped out of the car, laughing.

I followed her. "Well, I didn't really get to look at her face. But, whatever. She seemed pretty pissed. It was worth it, though. Chance is…well, you'll have to meet him."

"Oh jeesh. You just met the guy. How can you be that in to him already?" Jess rolled her eyes.

"I know. That's what's so crazy about it." I stepped faster to keep up with her. "I just met him but I feel like he's always been in my life. I don't know how or why but maybe I met him when I was younger or something. When he's around me it's like he's always been there. It's hard to explain." Great. I just did what I told myself I wouldn't— gushed to Jess.

"That's okay Lora. I think I get it." She winked. "Anything else major you haven't told me that I should know before we go into the bull pen?"

"Nope, I think that's it. If I remember anything more, I'll let you know." I laughed, thankful she was acting normal again.

We stepped into the old brick building and walked by the various groups of kids standing around the gym, catching up from the summer. I hated this place.

Once we got our schedules, we headed out to the hall to find our lockers.

The old, worn-down White Salmon High School had four brick buildings: a gym, an auditorium, a building that held both shop and music, and the main building. The main building had a center point that was the cafeteria. Surrounding the cafeteria were locker bays lining the walls with four main branches of long halls with various classrooms.

We found our lockers, separated by two locker bays, so we decided to share both of them. My locker kept the books for the first half of our day, while the second half of the day would be kept in Jess'. I wrote down both combinations in my notebook.

On our way to first period drama, we ran into Johnnie who seemed to almost be skipping. How cute. I don't know why Jess didn't like him.

"Hey Johnnie!" I said.

He hugged me and then pulled himself away and held my arms while looking at me and obviously forced his expression to be serious. His eyes laughed, though. "Tell me, Lora, is it true?" he asked all dramatic-like.

"Is what true?" I squirmed from his grip.

"There's a rumor going around that you have a new boyfriend—a boy of mystery." He couldn't hold his laughter any longer and Jess joined him, laughing it up at my expense. I stared at them, trying to look hurt by pushing my bottom lip out in a frown. I had to admit that it sounded rather humorous.

"A boy of mystery? Oh my gosh, Johnnie! Is that what people are saying?" I grinned and couldn't hold a small laugh. "First off, he is no *boy*. But yeah, not that it's anybody's business, I do have a boyfriend." Those words sounded weird.

Both Johnnie and Jess had way too much fun at my expense for the remainder of the morning. "Laugh it up now," I told them at lunch, "because you won't be laughing when you meet him."

"I'm looking forward to it." Jess winked.

"Yeah, me too! When do we get to meet this super boy?" Johnnie asked.

"I don't know. Depends on how lucky you are. Maybe we can all get together this weekend, like go to a movie or something?" I hoped, but then wished it back, because Chance may not like hanging around my immature friends.

The afternoon lasted forever. The first day of school was usually the most boring anyway because we had to go through all the introductions and rules of each classroom— like we all haven't been going to the same schools our entire lives.

Luckily I didn't have Dani in any of my classes and only saw her for a brief moment right after lunch. I dodged her and her entourage by hiding in a locker bay until they walked by. Lame. I cringed at the thought of facing her. Not that I had anything to worry about. If Chance liked her, he would have taken her to his place instead of me. It wasn't my fault he chose me instead of her.

School finally ended and I pushed Jess out of the locker bay so that we could leave.

"What's the rush?" she asked.

"Nothing, I just want to get out of here. Six hours is way too long to be here after having a break. I'm tired of it. Let's just go already!"

When we pulled up to Jess' house I tried as hard as possible not to shove her out of the car. "Okay then. Are you going to pick me up tomorrow morning?" I asked.

"You aren't going to come in?" She smirked, but I couldn't tell if she was serious or not. Probably serious.

"Oh, uh, I've got a lot of stuff to do and stuff and I wasn't planning on it today. Maybe we can hang out tomorrow or something?" I didn't want to hang out tomorrow either but I had to say something.

"Are you meeting Chance?" She didn't seem bothered by it.

"Yeah." I blushed and bit my lip. "I'd invite you to come over but I'm not sure what he has planned."

"'Kay. But I want to talk with you about something important, so maybe we can plan on hanging out for a bit tomorrow after school if that's okay with you?"

"Okay. I'll see you tomorrow morning then," I said.

Jess climbed out of the car. "Cool. See ya." She slammed the car door and headed toward the house, turning around when she got to the front door to give a wave. I honked and drove up the hill to my house.

I tried to calm my pulse as it sped with nervous anticipation. A few seconds later, I turned down my street and scanned the road for his Jeep. It sat on the side of the road in front of my house. Tingles flourished through my body.

Aubrey's Volvo sat in the driveway. She was supposed to be at work. I parked next to her and stepped out into the relentless gray afternoon.

Chance wasn't in his Jeep.

Eleven

I reached to open the front door but stopped mid-grab of the knob when Chance said, *I don't need your permission.*

I jerked around to find no one.

But if you care about her, you'll let her finish high school, I heard Aubrey say as if she stood next to me, but no one did.

A breeze blew the faded leaves in the tree, swooshing and swaying in the gray sky. A car splashed through puddles and kerplunked into dimples on the worn asphalt. The remainder of the world seemed to have vanished or hid from me; only the sound of trees and tires and then voices remained to keep me company in my isolated world.

She's not going to need to know any of that crap. We'll teach her everything she needs. Chance's voice had an edge to it I'd never heard before. He sounded angry.

Thump-thump, thump, thump. Thump-thump, thump, thump. Two heart beats echoed in my ears. One quick, the other slow. I squeezed my eyes shut and shook my head, trying to get rid of the voices and the beats and leaves and the water splashing. It didn't work.

I opened my eyes. Color no longer existed. Like before in the kitchen, everything turned to shades of gray. My breathing quickened.

Ask her first. I beg you to honor her wishes. Aubrey's voice trembled.

Fine! It's not up to me— His words came out as a growl. *Shh! She's home.*

A prickling sensation of someone watching me crawled up the back of my head. I zipped around to find Old Man Franklin duck out of his window across the street. Stupid snoop.

Only the heart beats continued. They blocked out all other sounds and they both sped up, one still racing faster than the other. I took a breath, blinked several times and then opened the door. Color filled my view. Yellow walls and brown carpets. The beats faded, replaced by the ticking clock. Tick-tock, tick-tock, tick-tock.

Aubrey sat on the couch with one foot tucked under her leg and Chance sat in the recliner next to the end-table. They both stared at me when I walked in. An eerie energy hung in the room. Crinkled brows and tense jaws vanished before my eyes. Chance's face clicked on. His smile erased all the tension. I swooned and sighed uncontrollably. He really needed to stop doing that.

"You didn't tell me you met someone, Lora." Aubrey winked at Chance. "He is absolutely charming."

"Duh. You've been gone." The attitude in my voice caused me pause and must have startled Aubrey too because her lips pressed together in her 'don't be a princess' look. "Sorry. Yeah. Chance meet Aubrey, Aubrey meet Chance. Happy?" Wow, someone smack me. Aubrey glared, then stood, stomped out of the room and mumbled, "Thanks," under her breath.

"How was school, Princess?" Chance asked in his smooth, deep voice.

"Long and boring and it wouldn't end, but finally, it did." I flopped on the couch near Chance. "Is there something you wanted to ask me?"

Chance nodded. "Let's go for a walk."

I jumped off the couch and hollered into the kitchen. "Going for a walk!"

"I suppose that's okay. Will you be home for dinner?" Aubrey asked.

"Would you like me home for dinner?"

"Yes."

"Whatever." I rolled my eyes, grabbed Chance by the hand and led him out the front door.

"Where do you want to go?" I turned around to ask Chance but he grabbed me by the arm and pulled me close. He squeezed me tight.

"What's wrong?" I asked with my face smashed against his chest.

I missed you.

My body went limp in his embrace. "I missed you more. You have no idea." I whispered back.

We stood like that for a few moments until the dark clouds above released their weight upon us. It wasn't a heavy rain, but just a little drizzle.

"Do you still want to go for a walk?" I asked, afraid he would say no.

Of course, my sweet. His thoughts in my head no longer seemed weird. The only thing that seemed weird to me was that all of these changes felt natural.

He took my hand. We walked up the street to the unmarked trailhead to my favorite place to write in my journal—my secret place. The trail led up the hill with beautiful views of the Gorge when the skies were clear. The ground slurped under our feet with every step. The only other sound came from the light rain making music on the umbrella of trees high above our heads.

Cool, moist air smelled of pine trees and earth. I held onto it with my lungs for a moment longer than normal with every breath. It felt peaceful and comforting to be with him, holding his hand.

Chance stopped and pulled me close again. Rain glittered on his dark hair and shimmered on his golden face from the small amount of light penetrating the forest. Holding my head with both of his hands, he leaned his face close to mine. His breath warmed my cheeks, slow and steady. Then it became labored and heavy. His gaze burned holes through my eyes. The world became a blur around me. My only focus was him. Nothing else existed, only Chance.

He tilted my face up to his. His lips brushed mine. The ground disappeared from under my feet, the sky no longer wept, the world no longer turned—life stood still—frozen in time with Chance holding me and kissing me. He was mine. Every part of my body came alive. Electricity surged through my limbs. My lips all the way down to my toes tingled.

He pulled away. *It's you I've waited all my life for, my sweet princess.* He kissed my forehead, then turned to walk again in comfortable silence.

We reached the turnaround on the trail where I would usually write in my journal whenever I wanted to be alone. Two logs on the ground made for good benches to sit on and acted as a barrier from the cliff on the other side. It dropped all the way down to the highway in front of the river. Sitting there during the summer time, one could look to the east to watch the sun rise in the morning and look to the west in the evening to watch the sun set. The towns became miniature models next to the mighty river down below.

Chance sat on one of the logs and tapped his hand next to him for me. The wet soaked into my jeans. It didn't matter though.

He caressed my knee and spoke, and he looked out over the Gorge. "There is something that I need to take care of and I need to do it now." A hint of sadness pinched his voice. "I'll need to go out of town for a few days, but I promise I will be back no later than a week from now." He turned, his eyes searching my face.

My heart sank. "Okay." I fought back the tears that threatened to spill if I let them.

"Or," he said. "You could quit school and come with me."

I laughed. He didn't. "What?" I asked.

"Move away with me. I'm needed at my home and want you to come with me."

"What does that have to do with quitting school?" I asked.

He chewed on my question for a few moments. He ran his hand through his damp hair. "We could travel the world." His gaze turned back to the twinkling lights of the towns below.

"Uh, sure, but I still need to finish high school."

"No, actually, you don't." His jaw clenched. "Where we're going, a diploma will mean nothing."

"Where are we going?" I tried to scoot away to get a better look at his expression, but my body stayed glued to the log.

"Listen, Princess." He rubbed his face vigorously and then blew out a chest full of air through his mouth. "Forget it. I'm sorry. Sometimes when I think about going home, I freak out a bit. Don't worry about it." He grabbed my hand and stood up. "Let's go."

I blinked away the blur that stung my eyes. Chance may've been the hottest guy in the world, but he needed a shrink. And I was no shrink, so I stood.

He pushed me. In return, I shoved him back using all my strength but he didn't budge, only laughed at me hysterically. I didn't think it was funny.

We walked back to the trailhead slower than our walk up the trail. This time he talked the entire way, telling me various stories from his long days spent windsurfing. Most of the stories he told made me laugh because they involved him hurting himself, which seemed comical at the time.

When we reached his Jeep, he kissed my forehead. "One week," he said out loud.

"One week," I said.

He squeezed me tighter, then released me. His hand grazed my cheek before he turned to go.

Forcing a smile on my face, I waved as he drove away. I didn't have to fight the tears any longer—they streamed down my face. I walked toward the house, thankful Aubrey's car was gone. Guilt jabbed my stomach at how I'd treated her. I'd never spoken that way to her before. Maybe I needed a shrink too.

The tears still hadn't stopped when I walked into the house and into the bathroom. I piled my wet clothes onto the floor then turned on the shower, letting the hot water run over my cold body. My sorrow mingled with the water and washed down the drain.

***

We pulled into Jess' lonely driveway after school. "Where are Mandy and Amy today?" I asked.

"They went to Seattle for a couple of days. Gallery stuff." Jess shrugged. Mandy and Amy often left Jess to fend for herself. We used to plan elaborate parties where we'd invite everyone we knew and rock out 'til dawn, but never went through with our plans because most the people we knew lived in the same town we did. And, well, enough said. Instead, we'd gorge ourselves to near death with every form of refined sugar and high-fructose corn syrup and the scariest movies available at Video Mart. I didn't think we'd be doing that tonight.

I marched straight to the couch and crashed. Throw-pillows felt like clouds under my head. "I don't know why I've been so freaking tired lately. I get plenty of sleep."

"Maybe you're getting sick or something. Are you taking your vitamins?" Jess asked.

"Yes, Mom." I sighed. "What's so important you wanted to talk about? Last time someone wanted to talk to me, he told me he was leaving. You aren't leaving are you?"

Jess sat on the chair across from the couch. "Not right away." Her expression remained blank.

"What?" I jolted up. "Serious? What do you mean not right away?"

"Let me start at the beginning." She held her hands up. "Don't say anything before I'm finished, okay?"

"Uh, 'kay." I lay back down.

"This past summer I went through a lot of difficult situations."

"Like what?"

"Hey, let me finish." Jess crossed her arms.

"Oh, yeah. Sorry."

She took a breath. "So, I didn't talk to you about anything because I was still going through it all in my head. I've been confused about a lot of stuff that happened—I'm sorry I was such a biotch when I got home." She paused a few moments, staring at the floor before she began again.

Thump-thump, thump-thump, thump-thump, thump-thump.

Jess' voice mumbled beneath the sound of the rapid heartbeat. Water filled a toilet tank upstairs, *shhhhhhshhhhhshhhh*. A wall heater kicked on, blowing warm air into the living room, *hummmmmm*. All color washed out of the stained-glass lamps, and then the light illuminating from them turned to a pale shade of gray. The walls, shag throw-rugs, hardwood floors, the chair Jess sat in, and even Jess became an old-fashioned TV show with no color and poor sound quality.

I watched as Jess' eyes blinked and her mouth continued to spill a muted version of slurred voice.

You're going insane, Lora. There's no doubt about it.

The world turned into an episode of 'The Twilight Zone' and all I could do was lay there and watch. It's too bad popcorn wasn't included in the price of admission.

Jess' brows furrowed and then her eyes bulged. She became silent.

My ears rang. Heat flushed through my chest and up my throat. Speak!

93

I forced words out. "So, you're telling me you're gay, right?"

Jess' mouth dropped open. "No. You didn't hear a word I said, did you?"

Color snapped back into the room like a commercial does before the credits finished scrolling up the screen. I sat up.

"But, yeah," she said. "I guess I am." Her gaze moved across the floor.

"You okay with that?"

"Psssh. Duh." I pushed the weirdness of my insane episode to the back of my mind where it belonged, locked away in a vault, to concentrate on the weirdness of the conversation. "Yeah. You're my best friend. Just don't kiss me again and we'll be cool."

She blushed. "Yeah, that was psycho, huh?"

"Psycho is an understatement." I flopped back down on the clouds covered with velvet fabric. "So, what were you saying before?"

She spoke again, but all I heard was the steady rhythm of her voice connected to no words. And then nothing. Black.

***

Dream Journal Entry: September 8th

Trees in the forest. Fog in the forest. Rain in the forest. Slurping mud beneath my feet.

An ivory gown draped from my shoulder to cling to my body and anchored itself in the ground; the rain and mud behaved like glue.

I sludged forward, using all my effort with every step to pull my feet from the earth and then dragged my anchor until I could go no further. I hit something hard. My hands went

94

up to touch a clear glass-like surface. An entire wall of invisible.

I traced my fingertips along the smooth barrier to find an edge, but didn't find one.

Someone appeared on the other side, just inches from the glass. She sort of looked like my dream mother in a way I'd never dreamt her. She wore an ivory gown clinging to her body from the rain soaking it to her skin. Mud caked the bottom up to about her knee. Black mascara ran from her eyes and down her cheeks as though she'd been crying. Water dripped from the blond hair hanging over her shoulders.

A man in black clothing and shimmering boots stood behind her, against a tree. His black hair slinked as long as my dream mother's and his white beard frizzed as long as his hair. Familiar clear eyes stared from his sockets right at me. Everything about him seemed familiar and gave me an uneasy feeling.

He smiled at me, exposing jagged gray teeth, and turned to step behind the tree where he disappeared.

I relaxed my shoulders and realized I'd been holding my breath when I blew a lung full through my nose. I stood there staring at my mother, her gaze as intense as mine.

Branches shook from the tree. A big shadow paced in the darkness just over the line where the light met the dark. And then it crossed the border.

As if reading my mind, Dream-Mother's eyes grew large and fear overcame her once-was-sad face. I pounded on the wall and screamed.

Dream-Mother's fist vibrated the glass and her mouth opened, exposing a shaking uvula sandwiched between two tonsils. My gaze moved to watch her fist. Her eyes followed mine.

I zipped around faster than my feet stuck in the mud and lost my balance. I fell. The mud was too heavy. I couldn't get up. The clear eyes of the giant bear, the same eyes that just belonged to a freaky dude, blinked.

***

"Lora? Lora, if you don't wake up I'm going to dump water on you!" Jess' voice said.

"I'm awake," I mumbled.

"Open your eyes then."

I let out a deep sigh and struggled to pry them open. The cool air stung and I blinked to end the dryness. I pulled a blanket that Jess must have put on me over my head.

"Sorry Jess. What were you saying?" I asked.

She laughed. "I seriously think you should go get a checkup."

I snorted. "Why?"

"It's time for school." Jess' voice was all serious.

"What?" I sat up and rubbed the sleep from my eyes. "Are you serious? Why didn't you wake me up?"

"I tried. You were a log and wouldn't budge. I called Aubrey and she said to let you sleep here. I even turned the TV real loud trying to wake you up." Jess laughed again. "You were totally boring, you know, and are lucky I didn't get bored enough to put whipped cream on your hand or something."

"I should go home to take a shower."

"I'll drive." Jess twirled car keys around her finger.

***

Dressed and clean, I headed toward the kitchen. "Want some cereal?" I yelled into the living room at Jess who sat on the couch.

"Sure." The TV clicked off and she stepped into the kitchen. She pulled bowls out of the cupboard.

"I just can't shake being tired." I said through a mouth full of Cheerios. "And then, on top of that, I miss Chance. It's insane because I just met the guy." I swallowed and took a drink of orange juice. "I don't know what's going on with me. The more I sleep, the more tired I am and with every minute that passes I want to see Chance again even more."

"I don't know. Like I said, you should go see a doctor. Especially over this Chance crap. What the hell?"

"I know!"

We finished eating, then went out the door for school.

The wet morning belonged to the land of tortoise, creeping by one small step at a time. All my classes ticked by in a muted haze. Falling asleep with my eyes wide open and thinking of Chance became my occupation.

"Lora, come on. It's lunch time." Jess smacked the arm supporting my chin on the desk. My head dropped. "We need to get some caffeine into you. I'll buy you a soda," she said.

I followed her out of the classroom, catching up to walk into the cafeteria together.

We froze in the entrance.

Without her entourage attached to her hip, alone with Johnnie, at our table, the same table we've claimed since ninth grade, sat Dani.

Twelve

"Oh, great," I said under my breath so only Jess could hear.

"I'll go get us some sodas." Jess bolted toward the vending machine.

I hesitated, then pivoted to leave.

"Lora!" Johnnie's voice boomed over the mumble of the cafeteria.

So much for escaping. I walked to our table and sat across from Johnnie and Dani. Johnnie watched me with a huge grin across his entire face.

"Hi guys." I tried to sound as natural as possible, but it came out with too much enthusiasm. I bit my lip and turned around to find what was taking Jess so long. Knowing Jess, she probably ditched me to go eat her lunch outside or in the bathroom or anywhere other than with Dani.

"Lora, you look like crap," Johnnie said. "Haven't you been sleeping at all? You're like a walking zombie." Abnormal concern lined his face, surprising me. It vanished though when Jess plopped down next to me with only two sodas. "You didn't get me one?" Johnnie's voice whimpered through a lace of hurt. I laughed. He kicked me under the table.

"Ouch!" I opened my soda and slurped it for him to hear then belched as equally loud, blowing it in his face.

"Nice." He jerked away with a grimace.

"Hey Dani, how've you been?" Jess asked. It seemed unnatural for her to be cordial to Dani. Almost forced.

"I'm fine I guess. I haven't seen you guys for a while. How are things?"

"Outside of Lora turning into a zombie, things are great." Jess grinned.

"I'm not turning into a zombie. Jeesh. I'm just tired, that's all."

Uncomfortable silence.

I belched toward Johnnie.

"Lora! You're so nasty." He plugged his nose.

I winked. "Paybacks buddy—"

"I want to ask you something," Dani said to me.

Glancing over at Jess who concentrated on her sandwich and then over to Johnnie who still grinned like a dork made me feel like reaching over and slapping them both. They didn't pay an ounce of attention as to what was happening. Dani could have bitten my neck and sucked the life out of me and they'd never have known what happened.

"Did you see me at the beach the other day?" Dani asked me with a slow, cautious tone.

I sent Jess signals with my eyes and willed her to pay attention. She continued to be more interested in the invention of PB&J. "Were you there?" I grasped for a life saver, but only found words. Lots of them. "I fell asleep for a while. I thought I saw you out of the corner of my eye when I was leaving but I was in kind of a hurry. I wasn't sure if it was you," I said in one breath and completely failed Lying 101. May I please be excused from the table now?

"Yeah, that was me. Did you happen to see who I was with?" She looked away from me, at the table, behind me and then back at the table again.

"No, like I said, I didn't even know it was you. Why?"

"I was with one of Chance's surfer friends, Julien. I think he's Chance's brother. He said he met you at the diner once." She paused. "Do you know who I'm talking about?"

Diner. Chance's friend. Hmm. "I'm not sure, Dani. There were two guys with Chance at the diner that day. I didn't really meet them, I just seated them." Maybe she wasn't mad about Chance after all and I was just imagining everything—wouldn't be the first time.

"Well, Julien is about six foot with blond hair and blue eyes. He's real cute." Her gaze moved to me. "That day at the beach was our second date. I was hoping you would come over to meet him but you were preoccupied I guess." Dani looked at the table.

"Okay. Yeah, I remember him. So, wait. You don't like Chance?"

"Chance is way too good looking, Lora. I'd have to worry about him with other girls. Too much stress." She rolled her eyes. Of course, just like her ex, Jason.

"Cool." I practically squealed and then cleared my voice. "I mean, that's awesome. So tell us about Julien."

Her face dropped further. "I was hoping you'd be able to tell me. He disappeared on Tuesday without a word. I'm worried, but at the same time pissed that he left without telling me. Do you know anything?" Her eyes glazed pink.

I told her how Chance left, too, and that he'd be back in a week. Julien sounded like a jerk. "Do you have his cell phone number?" I asked. "Maybe you should call him."

Dani sighed. "Yeah, I've tried that. He's not answering."

"It was kind of last minute. I wouldn't be angry until after he gets back and tells you what happened. Chance seemed to be in a hurry when he left. Maybe there was an emergency or something." Defending jerks usually wasn't something I strived to do on a daily basis, but Dani never behaved this needy before. Maybe she felt like I did about Chance. I'd totally freak out if Chance disappeared.

"Okay. Will you let me know if you hear anything?"

"Sure." I nodded.

Dani shuffled away with her head down. One by one, her entourage appeared from out of the woodwork. They seemed to replenish her super-cheerleader-powers. She pushed her nose to the ceiling and shoulders back where they belonged in the normal structure of things.

"I thought for sure she was going to confront me about *Chance*," I said once Dani was far enough she wouldn't hear me.

"Me too!" Jess and Johnnie said at the same time.

I rolled my eyes. "You guys would have liked to see that. Both of you just sat there and didn't help me out one bit."

"That's not true. I would have jumped in if it got physical and you were losing." Johnnie laughed.

"Whatever," I said under my breath.

When it came to cat fights, both best friends, my appendages so to speak, were fans. That's one thing they had in common. Although they would bet against each other as to who would win, they'd have a good time reminiscing about the action later. Especially if biting and scratching had been involved. The more blood the better. I'd like to think they would have agreed to bet against my opponent, but then I'd never been in a cat fight before. Never even close.

"We need to get you outside for a hike soon." Johnnie pointed at me. "You look like crap and need some fresh air or something." He had way too much enthusiasm.

"I don't know Johnnie. I'm not much of a fun person right now—I'm so tired. It takes all my effort just to go to school." I put my head down on my arms on the table. "Wake me up when lunch is over."

"I'm serious, Lora. Let's go hiking Saturday. We don't have to go far, just on one of the local trails or something."

"Yeah. Okay. Whatever, Johnnie. Now leave me alone." I closed my eyes.

"Do you want to go, Jess?" Johnnie asked.

"Can't. Gallery stuff."

All speak, all mumble, all noise faded and I drifted to dreamland only waking when the bell rang for the lunch hour to end.

The remainder of the week dragged. I slept an average of fifteen hours a day and it still wasn't enough. Aubrey didn't seem concerned. "You're just going through a hormonal change. It's normal," she had said.

Jess had an absolute fit and disagreed with Aubrey. She went as far as making a doctor appointment for me which I promptly cancelled. Johnnie thought I needed some exercise. Aubrey said it would be a good idea for me to get out as well. I didn't know what everyone's problem was. All I needed was sleep. Besides, when awake, the thoughts of Chance made me miserable. He hadn't called once since he left—not that I expected him to or anything—it just would have been nice. Sleep became my escape from the heartbreak of Chance's absence.

Thirteen

I spent Saturday morning alternating between unconsciousness and a state of vegetable, aware of my surroundings, but not active. Unconsciousness won the battle the majority of the time while I lay on the couch. It felt natural to keep my eyes closed and stay under the ten-thousand blankets piled on me.

The sun returned and rays of her far reaching arms seeped in through the window, heating the house further. I'd had the heater on all night, but it didn't matter because no matter how warm the house became, I still shivered—another hormone change according to Aubrey. My teeth chattered uncontrollably.

Chatter, chatter, breathe in. Chatter, chatter, breathe out.

Johnnie arrived on time. He let himself in through the front door.

"Get up Lora! Let's go," he said with a gruff voice and pulled layer after layer of warmth off me.

"Are you grumpy?" I mumbled, forcing my eyes to open.

"No, I'm not grumpy. I'm just sick of you constantly sleeping. Look at you—you're pale as a ghost. It even looks like you lost some weight. Have you been eating?"

He's grumpy. "Yes Johnnie! I *have* been eating. This isn't my fault, so don't be such a jerk. Aubrey says it's normal and that my mother even went through a phase like this." I rolled off the couch.

"Are you wearing that?" Johnnie's eyes traveled from my jeans up to my flannel shirt which covered two under shirts he didn't know about. "You'll be hot the second you walk out the door."

"I'm cold right now, but as soon as I warm up, I have a t-shirt on under this. Don't be such a worrywart. Okay?" I stomped out the door to the pickup.

"What's with the gun?" I asked, glancing at the handgun stuck behind the driver's seat. Johnnie sometimes carried his rifle with him during hunting season, but never a handgun.

"I'm bringing it just in case. There've been so many reports of wild animal attacks lately. It will be good to have if we need it, better to be safe than sorry." He sounded so sure of himself.

"Yeah—I suppose." I shuddered. I'd never touched a gun and didn't think I could shoot anything if my life depended on it. "Does your dad know you took his gun?"

Johnnie rolled his eyes. "Sure, Lora. If it makes you feel better."

No, it didn't.

Johnnie chose an easy trail across the river in Hood River, Oregon. It wasn't very long, but it had a waterfall at the end. The Wahclella Falls trail, an easy hike which made me extremely thankful. I yawned every few minutes the entire drive and became leery about how much energy I'd have to spend.

We pulled into the empty parking lot at the trailhead and parked in the spot closest to the trail. Johnnie grabbed the gun from the back when we got out of the pickup.

"Are you going to carry that while we're hiking?" The thought of him carrying a loaded gun freaked me out a little. What if he fell or something and the stupid thing blew his face off? Or worse yet—blew mine off!

"Lora, are you stupid? If there's a wild animal attacking us, do you think I'll have time to run all the way back here to get the gun then run all the way back to shoot it?" He fiddled with a thingy-majigy on the top. "Get that worried look off your face. I know how to handle a gun. Besides, I hunt all the time and I carry my rifle while I'm hunting. Duh."

"Is it loaded?" I asked.

"No. So don't worry about it." He stuffed it into the front of his shorts.

I couldn't tell if he was lying or not but took his word for it. We walked in silence along the trail. I conserved my energy for the walk by not talking. My lungs filled to the max with fresh, clean air, lifting the fog from my mind. It felt good to be outside. The warm sun beamed on my face, but the air held a chill that my flannel couldn't fight.

A bead of sweat ran down Johnnie's face and landed on his thin t-shirt.

I hoped my zombie-like self disappeared before Chance returned. He wouldn't want to hang around someone who looked and felt as dead as I did.

Maple trees lined the entire trail. In a few weeks, they'd be completely different trees with orange and yellow leaves falling to the ground. Kind of like me—changing and exfoliating into someone new. Hormonal changes were whacked.

We passed a sick looking maple tree. The branches drooped like rubber arms to the ground. Spots covered the trunk and the leaves had turned black. Sap seeped from the spots as though it wept in pain.

My knees buckled a few times along the way, becoming unreliable. I focused my eyes on the ground and counted each tedious step, following Johnnie up the trail and not paying attention to anything around us.

I ran right into Johnnie's backside. "Lora!"

"Oh, sorry." I poked him in the side with my finger. "Chill out."

"Be quiet for a second!" He scanned the forest. "Didn't you hear that noise?" His brows grew closer together.

"Nope, what did it sound like?"

"Like someone walking out there in the trees." He pointed out to the left, into the forest.

I supposed someone could walk out there but it would've been hard with all the ferns and vegetation.

"I didn't hear anything. Maybe it was a deer or something."

"Look," Johnnie whispered and pointed to two large spiders sitting on the wilting branch of another sick tree. "They're looking at us."

"Oooh. Scary." I chuckled. But, it was kind of weird. Not that anything hadn't been lately.

He searched the trees with his eyes a few more moments before continuing down the trail. I followed, allowing my thoughts to go back to Chance.

We left the forest area and wandered into a small opening that butted up against a stone cliff the water cascaded from. The mist from the falls billowed out several feet and left a thin film of moisture on our clothes. Freaking brrrrrr!

I leaned against a large boulder to rest for a few minutes. Johnnie set his gun next to a tree then kneeled on a rock next to mine. Sliding down off the boulder, I rested my head against it and sat on the rocky ground. It wasn't going to hurt anything to close my eyes for just a second. In fact, it felt wonderful.

The moisture turned into a thick fog around us behind my eyelids. It filled the entire open area, making it hard to breathe—a cold sauna. The fog swirled as if a wind blew it but I felt no breeze. I slowly opened my eyes to find that my imagination was reality.

"Johnnie?" I whispered.

"Yeah." Johnnie's voice came from right next to me but I could not see him.

"Where did all this fog come from?" I turned my head to find him and reached my hand out to feel him.

"What fog? I'm right here." He grabbed my hand, his skin moist and hot, and moved to sit closer to me to become a dark silhouette of Johnnie.

"You don't see all this fog?" My voice squeaked. Insane. Insane. Insane. Tears blocked-up my eyes.

A deep, raspy voice I had never heard before answered. *I see it. You're not going insane.*

I sat up abruptly. "Who is that?"

"Who is who?" Johnnie's voice was stern as if he talked to a naughty child.

"Nothing, I just thought I heard something." I took a deep breath to calm myself.

You did hear something. Not only was it something, but someone. Someone who has been searching the globe for you and now has found you.

I couldn't let Johnnie see the alarm I felt. He was already angry with my psycho behavior. Again, I took another breath and decided to think what I wanted to say. If I heard this person's words in my mind maybe he could hear mine.

Who are you? I spoke in my mind.

My name is Magiclure. I knew your mother and wish to know her still.

Johnnie tapped my shoulder and I jumped. "Lora, are you okay?"

"Just fine."

"Okay, jeesh!" He stood. "I gotta take a whiz. I'm going to those trees over there." He pointed behind us into the dense forest.

"Alright," I said, trying to control my irritability. Once he was gone I started up the conversation in my mind again. *Magiclure? Are you still there?* No answer. I sighed out loud.

"Yes?" I heard that outside my head with my very own ears. I searched around but the fog was still too thick that I couldn't see anything. A breeze blew a clear opening directly in front of me.

A familiar figure of a thin man stood in the trees. Long black hair, white beard, black clothing, and boots... The same man from my dream!

Is that you I see against the tree? I stood.

"Yes," he said.

My heart raced. I looked back to find Johnnie. My breathing sped up and I found it hard to control. I closed my eyes, concentrating on not hyperventilating.

Calm down Lora. Breathe in slowly. His voice didn't sound right but his words were kind. He was not kind in my dream. I didn't know if I should be afraid of him or not, but I was.

No. As long as you help me, there is no need to be afraid.

What do you want? I needed Johnnie to be here now.

I'm surprised Aubrey hasn't told you about me. He belted an evil loud laugh, sending chills down my spine.

How do you know Aubrey? My words sounded forced and fearful in my head.

"Like I said—I knew your mother..." His voice broke up.

Steps padded the ground from behind me. "Johnnie!" I screamed at the top of my lungs. Panic rushed through me.

You shouldn't have done that Lora. I don't want anyone to get hurt. He took a step forward. *Now calm down.* His fierce eyes glowed crystal clear in the dark forest ahead of me.

Another scream escaped my grasp.

He flashed out of sight. *I told you!* His voice turned to an anguished loud roar in my mind. Out of the darkness, a giant brown bear lunged from the forest right in front of me. He hovered several feet above my head while on all fours, staring and glaring at me with clear blue eyes. His upper lip curled in to show gray daggers embedding his mouth. Foam dripped from his lips.

You are making me very angry and I cannot control myself when I am angry. Please try to calm down.

More thoughts. No more thoughts!

"Stop it! Get out of my head. Just leave me alone."

The steps clapped closer and I swooshed around to see Johnnie heading my way. The fog had disappeared. He watched the ground in front of him.

"Johnnie!"

Johnnie froze in mid step. When he looked past me, his eyes just about popped out of his head. His hand went into the pocket of his shorts and pulled something out. He then sprinted for the tree.

I turned to face Magiclure. He continued to glare at me. His eyes not moving—locked with mine.

Lora, tell him to not pick that up.

"Johnnie, hurry!" I stepped backward, not taking my eyes off the giant bear in front of me. I tripped over a boulder and landed on my back.

Magiclure raised his front legs and stood on his hind legs, bellowing a loud roar. He was as tall as the trees. I tried to move my body, to stand up and run, but I couldn't. I couldn't move at all. I tried to scream, but nothing came out. I couldn't breathe.

A loud bang echoed through the forest.

I was finally able to scream again. I screamed and screamed and screamed. I couldn't stop, wouldn't stop. Ten million daggers stabbed my chest and just as many needles pricked inside my skull.

The gun had fired. Pain. My head rang. Unbearable pain burned through my chest and throbbed in my brain. Make it stop. Please.

Someone held my shoulders, rocking me. "It's okay Lora." Johnnie. "Open your eyes now. The bear is gone."

The daggers reduced to five down to three and to one stabbing my heart and then none. I opened my eyes. The needles in my brain melted away. Sitting up cautiously, I looked around. There was no fog. No bear. No Magiclure. Just me and Johnnie. He sat next to me, holding my arm. A pool of blood lay before us. Blood had splattered all over the boulders and bushes and even me. Patting my chest and my head to find the wound, I found none.

"What happened to Magiclure?" I whispered and scanned the trees.

"Who?"

"The bear? What happened to him?"

"He ran off. I got him pretty good in the chest but he turned and ran off into the woods. He probably won't make it very far before he bleeds to death. He was bleeding pretty badly." Johnnie's chest seemed a little more puffy than usual. He stood, pushed his shoulders back, and tilted his chin heavenward. "I told you the gun may come in handy."

"Thank you Johnnie," I whispered again. "I was almost that bear's dinner."

"No problem. Let's get you back. Do you think you can stand up?" He held me steady when I braced the boulders to help me up. A wave of extreme fatigue enveloped my body and I almost collapsed, but he caught me.

"I'm fine. Let's get out of here." I held my own and followed Johnnie to the trail. We stopped several times so I could rest, taking about three times as long to get back to the truck as it did going up to the falls. Johnnie was patient the entire way.

It was so difficult to keep my eyes open. I watched the ground, one foot stepped in front of the other. Occasionally, I closed my eyes for a moment or two. When I started to drift, my head jerked up. Then I shook it back and forth because

112

everyone knows that shaking your brain keeps it awake longer.

The events of today blurred into my thoughts like a dream at the cusp of forget. When we arrived home, Aubrey's car sat in the driveway. Weird. She usually wasn't home at that time of day. I looked down at my watch to find it was 5:30 PM and I wondered how it could be so late. She waited for us at the front door for some reason. I couldn't make myself understand what was happening. And then, she ran toward us.

Fourteen

I slowly pulled myself out of the truck. My weak legs almost buckled. Both Aubrey and Johnnie were at my side now, helping me into the house. Aubrey panicked when she noticed the blood splattered on my clothes. Johnnie assured her that it wasn't mine—it was the bear's blood. That didn't seem to calm Aubrey much.

"Is the bear dead?" she asked Johnnie.

"Not when we last saw him, but I'm pretty sure he will bleed to death. I got him right in the chest and he was bleeding pretty badly when he hobbled away." There was pride in his voice once again.

"Tell me everything." Aubrey's eyes almost bugged out of her head.

I crawled into bed and blacked out as soon as my head hit the pillow.

***

Far away voices inched closer as time slipped by. Although I couldn't understand the words, I knew the voices.

Strong scents and perfumes mingled in the room. They were so strong I fought to the surface to investigate the aromas.

The voices became louder and soon I understood some of the words. Just a few here and there like a foreign language with small interruptions of English sprinkled throughout the conversation. The backs of my eyelids glowed red.

Someone held my hand. Chance. The voices stopped but the strange scents stayed. Chance stroked my hand, then his hand moved to my head, combing through my hair. I smelled him stronger than I ever had before. A small laugh in my mind—his laugh—as if he read my thoughts.

Other scents arrived. One was almost floral, like fresh roses in the garden with a tinge of cinnamon. Aubrey. Oh, Aubrey. *What is it I needed to ask you?* There was something. Someone I needed to speak with you about. It escaped my memory right then.

A new scent entered, similar to Chance but different and much fainter. It wasn't as sweet, almost a bit sour. Again, the laugh plagued my mind. Oh, how I loved Chance's laugh. His lips landed on my forehead.

I tried to move my arms to hold him closer to me but they only twitched—too weak to move, too weak to hold my love. Sadness overwhelmed me and I struggled to open my eyes. They were heavy but I did manage to open them only to be blinded by light and closed them immediately.

Chance spoke with his chocolate voice, "Patience, my sweet. Rest some more." But I didn't want to rest anymore. I was resting way too much lately. My love was home and all I could do was lie there like road kill.

I will be here when you wake. I promise. You need to rest now.

I protested silently, using all my strength to move my arms. When I got them halfway up to where I thought Chance was, they shook. I had never been so weak in my life! Chance grabbed my arms and wrapped them around his

115

neck. He stretched out next to me. Yes, that was all I wanted. Comfort. Love. I drifted off once again.

My eyes opened on their own. The room was dark except for a stream of light coming from the hall through my cracked door. I sat up in bed and looked around. The little digital clock on the stand read 1:15 AM.

I didn't need much time to adapt to the darkness. In fact, I saw everything in my room as clear as day. Zero laundry scattered the floor and everything was in its place. Someone must have tried to be helpful.

Somehow I sensed movement in the living room. Three distinct scents lingered in the house. Chance, Aubrey, and someone I couldn't place.

The house was silent. Aubrey and newbie slept. I could tell by the sound of their breathing. Chance, on the other hand, he was listening for me.

Very impressive.

I sprang from bed a new person, full of strength and energy. Someone must have pumped me with whatever they fed that pink battery bunny that kept going and going and going.

Chance stood at the end of the hall. I ran into his arms and he embraced me tight. He kissed my forehead and I melted, suddenly weak again.

He laughed softly in my ear. "You, my sweet, are very lucky to be alive, and I am even luckier to have you alive."

I tried to recall the events of the last few days. All I could remember was being so tired all the time and of him leaving.

"It will come back to you in time Lora. Let us just enjoy this time together, shall we? Are you hungry?"

The answer to this question was an easy one. "Yes, I'm starving!"

"What would you like to eat?"

The words just came to my mouth with no thought behind them at all. "Steak! I would like a bloody rare steak!"

"I thought you would say that."

In the kitchen, Chance pulled my chair out for me. "For you." He bowed when I sat down.

"Uh, thanks?"

He pulled two large plates wrapped with tin foil from the oven. Before he ripped the foil off, I smelled what they were. Potatoes. He pulled a covered plate from the refrigerator. Bloody red meat. The metallic scent permeated the room. My mouth salivated and for some reason excitement surged through me. I had an urge to rip open the covered plate and start gnawing on the flesh.

"You spoiled my surprise." Chance's half-grin covered his lips. His eyes sparkled with approval.

Chance seasoned then seared the steaks on both sides using a frying pan. The whole cooking thing was torture. He then slapped each steak on a plate and added a potato before bringing the plates over to the table, placing one in front of me and the other was for himself.

The blood red juice from the steak ran over the entire plate when I cut into it. It was the best steak I had ever tasted. Not that I had steak often before. I hated meat. What the hell was wrong with me? Maybe I was just super hungry and anything would have tasted so good. I sopped the blood up with the potato.

When we both finished, I sprang from the table, grabbed the dishes, and rinsed them in the sink. The energy was awesome. It was about time I got back to normal but that was beyond normal. Never had dishes been washed so fast. I probably set a world record or something.

"Now what?" I shrugged. "Do you want to go somewhere?"

"There is nothing open this late, Princess. We can go outside if you'd like. Maybe go run off some of your energy?"

My body practically exploded while I ran next to Chance. Before that night, I hated running. It was evil. The worst form of exercise on the face of the planet. Yet, there I was, flipping running. Not just jogging either. Full-on, in your face, super-charged running.

The light from the streetlamps showed the only evidence of the rain falling. It was such a light drizzle, I couldn't feel it until my clothes were soaked through. The night was silent with the exception of our feet treading on the wet pavement. The cool, moist air in my lungs felt exhilarating.

Whenever we passed a house on the street, scents, images, and sounds of the people inside flashed in my head. It usually began with a faint smell that grew stronger as we approached. Each scent was very distinct and different from the others. Then the sounds came. Most houses only had the heavy breathing of sleep. Some had television or radio noises. An image of the interior of the house followed when we were directly in front of the house. I usually saw people sleeping but on occasion, just an empty room flashed in my head.

"Chance, what is going on?"

"You'll know all in the morning, my sweet." He winked at me and challenged me by running ahead. Oh that did it—I didn't know what it did, but I ran faster to catch up to him.

Pretty much all physical activity had been avoided at all costs before then. If I had known how amazing it felt to be a bullet through the air, I would have picked up this running gig ages ago.

Challenging myself, I ran faster, passing Chance. The rain pricked my face. Chance caught up with me, glancing over to my direction with a pinch of humor in his expression. Chance followed my pace and we stopped at the end of town. Blood coursed through my body—every muscle felt alive and full of energy.

We headed south on a narrow trail until we reached the train tracks that ran parallel with the river. We jogged at a slow pace down the tracks for quite some time in silence. The river caressed the shore. My mind raced while grasping all the changes I felt in my body. I'm sure Chance was reading my mind, but I didn't care. I wondered if I could read his and tried. He looked over at me as if he knew what I was trying to do.

Tomorrow, my love.

A heavy sigh escaped me. He stopped jogging and pulled me to a stop, putting his warm arms around me. I burrowed my head into his strong chest. The familiar feeling of extreme comfort overwhelmed me. Just then, I wanted to collapse in my bed again.

We ran back to the house in no time and went straight to my bedroom where he kissed my cheek and told me to rest before leaving to let me change.

I slithered into my soft sweats and climbed into my warm bed. Chance came in with an extra blanket and sat in the rocking chair in the corner, covering himself. "Goodnight, my sweet Lora."

My eyes were heavy and soon I was gone.

I awoke to darkness. Alert and once again full of energy, I sat straight up. The clock read 9:00 PM. My new senses told me the same three people that were here last night were still here, but this time they were all waiting and talking amongst each other. They were then silent for a split second.

"She's awake," Chance said.

Fifteen

After taking care of some much needed shower time, I headed to the kitchen to devour every morsel in sight.

Lit candles peppered the counter tops, causing the kitchen to glow warm. Three people sat at the table, and eggs, bacon, and more bacon were heaped in mounds on a plate in front of the empty seat. Yes. So. Hungry.

"Good evening, Princess!" Chance beamed at me.

"Hi!" I wanted to run to him, to hold him, but that felt awkward with the others sitting so close. Instead, I walked in and sat down in the empty seat and hovered over the dead pig and chicken embryos like a vulture.

"This smells delicious!" I said.

"Help yourself, Lora. I'll get you another plate if you'd like. I wasn't sure how much to make but it is all for you if you want it." Aubrey pushed the plates further toward me.

"That's a lot of food just for me, but to tell you truth I'm so hungry I could probably eat it all." I shoveled a fork full of scrambled eggs into my mouth along with two pieces of bacon. "Mmm, this is so good." I chewed and then chomped into another piece of bacon. "You know, I could have been enjoying all these dead animals my entire life. No freaking wonder people eat them."

I looked up, still stuffing my face, at everyone and found three pairs of eyes staring at me. A loving brown pair belonging to Aubrey and two pairs almost an identical shade of crystal clear blue. Chance and that other dude Dani liked. I couldn't remember his name…

Chance's face turned pink. "This is my brother, Julien." His hand gestured toward Dani's guy.

"It's a pleasure to meet you, Lora." Julien nodded. He was beautiful. Not nearly as beautiful as Chance, though. He looked a lot like Chance, but with blond hair. His shoulders were broader and his jaw slightly more angular.

"Hi Julien." More yummy eggs. Eggs. Who would have thought eggs would be so freaking good? "Oh, and my friend Dani told me that if I were to see you, to have you call her."

"Thanks for the message."

Aubrey and Julien pushed back from the table and then went into the living room. The television flicked on. News.

Chance reached for me, pulling me tight to him.

"Finally!" I sighed.

I heard his hushed laugh in his chest as he kissed the top of my head. "Eat. Your stomach is still rumbling."

"I know. It's crazy."

I stuffed the last piece of bacon into my mouth when Aubrey and Julien came back into the kitchen. Aubrey picked up my plate and went to the sink.

"How do you feel?" she asked.

"Amazing! Is anyone going to fill me in on what's going on with me? Do I need to go see a doctor? One week I'm exhausted and sick then the next I have a ton of energy and my senses are weirding out. I can smell things I never noticed before, even see better than ever. Then there's the fact that my memory isn't good at all. I can't even remember what day it is. Oh, and sometimes, the color just, like, disappears out of everything!"

Aubrey took a deep breath and slowly let it out while looking at Chance. Chance nodded at her as if he was giving her the encouragement to continue.

"Lora, there are things about you that have been kept a secret. I want you to keep an open mind and be patient with me. This is hard to explain so that you'll understand completely." Aubrey dried her hands on a towel and sat at the table across from me. "First, I'll start out with what you are. Then we'll move on to where you're from and who you are." The skin on her forehead puckered as her eyebrows closed together in concentration.

"Don't worry, Lora. Just listen." She then gestured to the living room. "We'll be more comfortable in the other room."

Chance and I sat next to each other on the couch while both Aubrey and Julien sat in recliners. Candles illuminated this room too, making everything that much more surreal. Orange flames devoured a log in the fireplace.

I wrung my sweaty hands together. Chance grabbed them and held on tight.

"First, to answer your question about the date—it is Wednesday, October 1st." Aubrey paused to let that sink in.

My mouth dropped open. The last I remembered was the first week of school in September.

"You look bewildered." Aubrey scooted to the edge of the recliner and leaned toward me. "You have been in and out of consciousness for almost a month…since the attack."

The attack? What attack? I looked from Aubrey to Julien to Chance.

"The bear?" Aubrey said like a question.

Bear, bear…there was something about a bear. I couldn't remember what, though.

Chance interrupted my thoughts. "You were attacked by a bear the day you went hiking with Johnnie. Johnnie shot the bear and brought you home."

A horror filled my entire body, slowly creeping down into my limbs as the memory of that day came filling my mind all at once. Gray and pointy teeth. Horrific breath. And the blood. "Magiclure," I whispered.

Chance jumped to his feet. "What did you say?"

"Magiclure?" I asked.

"Where did you hear that name?" Aubrey said in a panic and moved to the couch, sitting next to me, her face inches from mine. I looked up at Chance and back to Aubrey. Anticipation filled their faces.

It took several moments to recount the memory to them. When I finished, the room fell silent, but for the crackling of the fire.

"We didn't know Magiclure was near," Chance finally said. "He's dangerous and has been missing for as long as your mother." He sat back down and looked at Julien. "We're going to have to alert the others."

Julien nodded.

Aubrey grasped my hand. "You've been raised in a world and with a species that believes they are superior to everything on the planet. They believe they know everything there is to know and close their eyes and hearts to everything else. They see only what they know. But, in reality, there's so much more right in front of their eyes.

"You come from a world that was created thousands of years ago in a time when other intelligent creatures roamed Earth alongside humans. Although you still live with humans, they do not believe in your existence, which is how your species prefers it."

I pulled my hand from her grasp and stood. "What do you mean your species? I'm a freak or something?" I paced the floor.

Chance said, "We are a bit freaky."

Julien laughed.

I snapped my gaze to Chance. "What are you talking about? You're like me?"

We are the same, Princess. Chance said in my thoughts.

"Oh my god! Get out of my head. What the hell? Are we like psychics or something?" My footsteps stomped louder on the floor. Back and forth. My heart raced faster than anyone's in the room. Aubrey's beats thumped the slowest. Our hearts became a percussion practice session in my head. "And you," I pointed at Aubrey, "are different than us all."

"Just sit down, Lora. Let me finish," Aubrey said.

I sat in the recliner that time, away from the real freaks on the couch. I wasn't the freak. They were.

"You were born into royalty of this magical world. Princess Sabrina of Theriania is your mother, and Prince Oryan of Takoda, is your father. They were betrothed to each other at birth and were married on Sabrina's eighteenth birthday. This marriage united the two strongest tribes of your kind. There are three tribes or lands your kind dwells in: Theriania, Takoda, and Hornbrood."

"What the hell? What lands? I never heard of those lands before. What? From, like Pluto or something?" I pushed forward to the edge of the recliner.

Aubrey sighed. "Just listen. Hornbrood is an evil tribe that seeks to destroy both Theriania and Takoda. The leader of the Hornbrood tribe, Lord Xifan, has been trying to weasel his way into ruling all of the therianthropes for centuries now. That is what you are, Lora—a therianthrope. Some prefer the term shapeshifters."

I pointed at the couch where Chance and Aubrey sat and snapped my fingers. "I know that name! Xifan." From my dreams. My mind stung. I had no idea what fairytale Aubrey was talking about because none of it made sense. "Yeah and you're just a little bit insane if you think I'm a shapeshifter."

Chance leaped up again and paced the floor. "How do you know that name, Lora?"

I've never been one to allow someone to talk down to me, so I stood too. "Don't take that tone with me, *Chance*."

He drew a breath and released it. He rubbed his temples. *Sorry, my sweet.*

I rolled my eyes, not sure if I should let my guard down again or not. Julien just sat there with a grin on his face, eyeballing me. "What's his problem?" I nodded toward Julien. "Doesn't he speak or does he just sit there like a stupid idiot all the time?"

Julien laughed, exposing his brilliant white teeth. What was it with their teeth? OMG gorgeous.

"Lora, sit down." Aubrey's voice turned stern. "Let me finish."

I slumped back into the chair and sulked. Whatever. I was a freak from la-la land. Might as well do as I was told.

Aubrey arranged her legs into a pretzel on the couch. "A therianthrope is a shapeshifter. You can take on many animal characteristics in your human form such as heightened senses and speed. Some more than others depending on their breeding. Chance is a pure blood—as are you. You are the purest of any of the therianthropes." She paused. "Pure bloods are direct descendents of our very first royal family.

"You usually start the change in your late teenage years. Your form is that of human and all your characteristics are human until you are able to make the change. A normal change takes anywhere from a week to a few months. Weakness, fatigue, body aches are all normal at the beginning."

I laughed. "Well that explains everything."

No one else laughed.

"Sorry," I said. "Jeesh."

Chance winked at me and half-smiled. If I didn't know about all this freak business, I probably would have swooned, but now it just irritated me even more. He was so dang hot, after all, and I was trying to concentrate.

"So why has all this been kept from me?" I asked, humoring them.

"I'm getting to that, Lora. Please be patient," Aubrey said.

"Ahhh! Oh my gosh. This is taking forever. Just get to it already!" I was never the patient type.

"Princess Sabrina was Magiclure's best friend. They'd been friends forever. She had a way of calming him because he didn't have much control over his animal instincts. When Princess Sabrina turned eighteen, she was married to your father as planned, uniting the two tribes. Your father, now Lord Oryan, prohibited the friendship between Sabrina and Magiclure. I think it was more out of jealousy that Magiclure had a relationship with your mother stronger than your father could ever have with her.

"You were born a year later. It was a joyous occasion. Both tribes celebrated with a parade and feast. On the evening of the feast, your father went missing. Both tribes searched the lands. They eventually discovered him dead in the forest. All fingers pointed to Magiclure but he was nowhere to be found. Some people believed that he fled to join the Hornbrood tribe. No one knows for sure.

"Rumors began that your mother may have been part of the plot with Magiclure—which was ridiculous! But threats against her life made their way around the palace. No one could trace them to anyone. Out of fear for her life, as well as yours, we fled with you here. Once we arrived to White Salmon, your mother began to make the change. She was a late bloomer but it only lasted two weeks.

"We lived here together until your first birthday. Soon after, your mother disappeared."

Chance stretched his arms out in front of him and then cleared his throat. "I was born into the Takoda tribe. My parents were next in line for the lordship when your father was murdered. Your family and my family are the last of the pure bloods. Only pure bloods can rule our tribes—it is tradition. I, too, was betrothed to someone when I was a toddler. She was of the Theriania tribe and went missing when she was an infant." He swallowed hard. His clear eyes burned into my soul as he searched my mind to find my thoughts, but I had none. I only felt… lost all of a sudden.

Chance tried on his devastating half-smile again. That time, it worked to calm me instead of irritate me. "After my change, I searched the world for the one I was betrothed to. Our tribes were falling apart as Lord Xifan plotted to take over both Theriania and Takoda. Your grandfather's health is ailing. He has been standing in as Lord of Theriania until the rightful heir returns." His voice faded.

"This past year I almost gave up. I actually did give up when I found you. You, this beautiful girl whom I first saw last June hiking with your friend, Johnnie. We were prowling in the forest just for fun when I spotted you. I've been following you all summer long.

"When you finally noticed me at the gas station and then in the diner, my heart practically burst in my chest." *You don't even know what you do to me.* He looked around the room and then at the carpet.

Julien and Aubrey stood and went into the kitchen.

Chance moved to the recliner next to me, his knees brushed mine as we swiveled to face each other.

After being with you for one afternoon, I knew you were my soul mate. No longer did I care about my betrothed. No longer did I care I was to be lord when my betrothed came back. I didn't want her to come back for selfish reasons.

His face began to glow. *I had suspicions. Your fatigue concerned me and your birthmark on your arm— I had heard that royalty of Theriania had birthmarks like yours, but I had never seen one. I pushed it all out of my mind. I just didn't want to think about it I guess. Once I met Aubrey, I put everything together. I sensed she was a witch as she sensed me.*

"Wait a second! Aubrey's a witch?"

Chance laughed. "Yeah. There's a lot of this world you don't know about, Lora."

"Apparently."

129

When I left that day, it was because I had to deliver the news that you had been found and will be returning soon. You, Lora, my soul mate, are my betrothed!

That was the first thing that made sense all night. Yes, I could see being married to my Chance—my, uh, prince.

Aubrey piped up just then from the kitchen. "Oh, by the way, your birth name is Loramendi."

"What?" I asked. "Loramendi?"

Chance shook his head. "I don't know what to make of the timing with Magiclure showing up and all the strange animal attacks in the forest." He glanced at Julien who now stood in the doorway.

"Uh, hello? Why didn't anyone ever tell me my name was Loramendi and not just Lora? You couldn't have at least told me my real name?" I rolled my eyes.

"To keep you safe, hun," Aubrey hollered.

Whatever.

Julien crossed his arms. "I still believe it would be safest to take her to Theriania now. She can be protected there." This was the most I had heard Julien say at one time. His voice almost sounded like a bass guitar.

"I thought the bear was dead. Didn't Johnnie shoot him?" My voice raced out of me.

"There was no body found." Aubrey squeezed past Julien and sat back on the couch. "So we have to assume he's still alive. It takes more to kill shifters than it does humans." She turned toward Julien. "No one knows she's here. I don't think Magiclure means any harm—he has never meant anyone any harm. Let me find him and speak with him. After all, I practically grew up with him. I know him." Aubrey was firm in her decision.

It looked like Chance would back her up too when he nodded in agreement. I felt grateful for that. It gave me time to let all the crazy, fantastical stuff sink in. Maybe it would make sense later. Maybe not.

"What about Jess and Johnnie? Haven't they been around to ask about me?" I asked.

"They have both been very concerned," Aubrey said. "Either showing up or calling every day. Mr. Estes sent a message that he's holding your job for as long as you need. They think you are still in shock from the bear attack."

Aubrey opened her mouth to say something else when Chance snapped his attention to her, his eyes fierce. She laughed and said, "Oh, I forgot what I was going to say. Anyway…"

I wanted to ask more, but fatigue suddenly overwhelmed me and once again my eyes became heavy. Chance picked me up gently and carried me back to bed.

"This is all so crazy." I whispered in his ear.

"I know, Princess. I will answer all your questions when you wake. You need to sleep now. It shouldn't be too much longer—sleep, my love."

My eyes closed. Chance set me on the bed and lay down next to me. I snuggled close to him, breathing in his comforting scent. I couldn't wait to wake up and have this all be one of my dreams to write about in my journal in the morning. But for that, I had to dream some more…

Sixteen

It really irritated me that whenever I woke up it was dark outside. I craved sunlight. Fall was my favorite time of year and I was pretty much missing it. Walking through the crunchy leaves while breathing in the cool crisp air were things I yearned for all year long.

"It'll soon be over." Chance brushed my messy bed-head hair away from my face. "You'll get to see the sun again, Princess. Maybe you'll be up during the day tomorrow and we can go for a walk."

"What about Jess and Johnnie?" I asked. They had to be freaking out by then.

"We can see about that, too." Chance pulled my arm. "Get up. We need to get out of this house and get some fresh air."

"Where are we going?"

"After you get dressed and eat, let's go down to the beach and build a fire. The skies are clear and there is a cool autumn breeze. We can count stars or something." His voice held a hint of sarcasm.

"But, there is so much I still want to know," I said.

"You can ask anything you want when we get to the beach."

"Cool. Let's go, then!" I jumped out of bed, flinging my blankets across the room and ran to the bathroom to get cleaned up.

I studied the mirror carefully while brushing my teeth. The reflection wasn't me. It still looked like me, but my skin was paler, even smoother. My hair seemed much longer and thicker than before, and my eyes were a darker shade of brown with... "What the—" I leaned closer to analyze my eyes further.

"These aren't my eyes!" I threw open the door to find Chance on the other side. "Why didn't you tell me my eyes are changing? They're covered with blue flecks or something. Is this normal?" I stretched the lids open as far as they would go.

"Let me see here." Chance held my face with both hands and peered into my sockets. He wore his stupid half-grin which wasn't helping the situation at all. "Why yes, Loramendi, I do see quite a change. It appears you are turning into a...gasp...shapeshifter. Dun, dun, dunnnn."

I smacked his hands away. "Not funny. Am I going to have eyes like yours?"

"I'm afraid so."

"What? That's crazy. Do you all have the same color of eyes?"

He nodded.

I poked my finger in my eye to fish out whatever contact lens they had put in there while I slept. Ouch. No lens.

The more I studied the reflection, the better I liked the blue coloring. I gave myself a little wink and then I walked out of the bathroom.

Chance chuckled.

"Where is everyone?" I asked when I sat at the table.

"Aubrey should be back later tonight. She's been searching for Magiclure with no luck. Julien went back to

133

Takoda. He's going to bring back reinforcements. He thinks it's necessary, but I don't."

The blood drained from my face.

"Calm down, my princess. I won't leave your side." He pushed a plate with some kind of flesh toward me. "You're safe with me, I promise. Julien is just overcautious and protective." He grabbed my hand from across the table and squeezed.

"Now eat!" he said.

"Why don't you eat, too? I feel like a pig always scarfing down right in front of you while you just sit there, watching."

"Is there something wrong with being a pig?" He snorted and squealed.

"No way. Can you turn into a pig?"

"Yep. Would you like to see? I don't prefer to turn into animals we use as food, but would be happy to demonstrate for you."

A sickening sensation rose in my abdomen. "I don't think I can take that right now." It was bad enough I craved eating the poor creatures. Not to mention I didn't want to embarrass him when he couldn't actually turn into a pig. He was so serious about the shapeshifting stuff.

"I'm sorry, Lora. When you're ready, we'll explore the possibilities. It really isn't bad when you get used to it."

Looking down at the heaping pile of food, I realized what it was—pork chops! My stomach rumbled and saliva pooled in my mouth. I listened to my body, against my will, and shoveled the animal into my mouth. Delish. Gross. Gah! I was so confused.

134

Chance drove us to Lyle. We followed the cobblestone boardwalk, but instead of going to the house, we walked past it a short way until we reached an opening in the tall grasses that led to a trail to the river.

The cool and crisp night air that would usually chill me felt good against my warm skin.

We stepped over larger boulders. Feral cats darted into cracks between the rocks. They watched from their safe dark holes as we made our way, gracefully, down to the river.

Chance stopped at a sandy area where he had already set up a fire pit with a pile of wood that could last us all night. He opened a tin box already waiting for us near the wood and pulled out two fuzzy blankets and newspaper. He stacked the blankets on one of the two lounge chairs with soft cushions. I sat on the other and wrapped myself in the blanket. Chance built a fire.

In no time, flames blazed high into the sky. He stood back, admiring his accomplishment. I laughed.

"What? Can't a guy be proud of his fire?" He said while making manly grunts and pounding his chest.

He squished close to me in the lounger and wrapped his arms around me.

Millions of stars illuminated the sky. We listened to the crackling fire and the river lapping on the rocks. The peacefulness of it all felt so natural—I didn't want that evening to end. I didn't want to feel the exhaustion that put me in a coma for days at a time. Every cell of my body felt alive and I treasured the moment. I snuggled my face deeper into Chance's strong chest and breathed in his earthy scent. He squeezed me tighter.

I cocked my head sideways. "Chance?"

"Yes, my sweet?"

"What's it like in Takoda, where you're from?"

"It's hard to describe." He took in a breath. "All our lands are magical in a human sense. They were created by magic and are protected by magic. All three lands are in another dimension and remain hidden to humans. The portal to Takoda is in the Ural Mountains of Russia.

"Our lands are sanctuaries for other creatures or what you may call mystical creatures to dwell in as well."

I squirmed free from his embrace to get a look at him. "What kind of creatures? Like unicorns and stuff?"

Chance rolled his eyes. "No. Unicorns have been extinct for hundreds of years." He pulled me close to him again. "Orcs and elves and fairies and shapeshifters."

"Ha! Whatever." Sweat formed on my skin. I kicked the blanket to the ground.

"Takoda is completely different from Theriania. They used to be the same with ancient castles and rock huts, but Theriania was destroyed in 1980 so the magicians rebuilt the buildings."

"What happened? Did they blow it up or something?" I snort-laughed.

"Mt. St. Helens erupted," Chance said all serious.

My mouth dropped open in surprise. "The portal to Theriania is here in Washington!" That was meant to come out as a question but sounded more like an accusation.

"Yep. The forces of the eruption were so strong that they impacted our dimension as well, causing a massive earthquake and most buildings to come crumbling down to the ground.

"I grew up in a stone cottage just outside of the palace in Takoda. My nursemaid, Mrs. Olsen, raised me. Each of my brothers had separate nursemaids and we all grew up in separate cottages. My parents were rarely around. It gets boring in our realm, so we travel to the human realm a lot.

"All three of my brothers and I started training at an early age for combat. We learned everything there is to know about war and fighting in order to defend our lands from the Hornbroods—Lord Xifan in particular. If there's ever an attack, we are always on alert and ready to defend."

I pushed away and sat in the open chair to see him better. "This is all crazy, Chance. Is there going to be a war or whatever it is shapeshifters do?"

He chuckled and then got serious again. "There is an impending feeling that we will see war in our lifetime. We seem to be on the verge of something big, Lora. Our marriage will unite our lands, creating a force that Lord Xifan could never come up against. There was a joyous outcry when I delivered the news that you had been found."

"Wait. What?" My heart stopped thumping. The fire stopped crackling and the river stopped lapping. "Married?" I whispered. "Unite lands? Lands with fairies, no less."

He moved from his chair and sat next to me. "Married," he whispered. His sweet breath felt warm against my face. Tingles shimmered in my belly and traveled across my skin. His moist lips pressed against mine. The gods pressed 'pause' on the world while I made out with this gorgeous Chance. My Chance. Of course I'd marry him.

He slowly pulled away. "We'll live anywhere you want. If you want to travel the human realm, then that is what we'll do. But, we will still have the obligation of returning to our land when we are needed. We still must be responsible."

I thought I could live with that. Traveling the real word and returning to the fantasy world on occasion. That was, if there was such thing as a fantasy world.

Chance threw more wood on the fire. Sparks danced into the sky, reminding me of fairies. I wondered if they'd look like little embers dancing in the air.

We stayed on the beach for a couple hours, silently listening to the waves and the crickets making their nighttime serenade. Thoughts raced through my mind—my world had changed in a matter of days.

I missed Jess. A small pain stabbed my heart at the thought of seeing her again for the first time in so long, worrying about what she may think. I *do* look different.

"I'm hungry, again," I said after my stomach rumbled.

"I know." Chance grinned. "We have several options here. The first one is experimenting with some of your new abilities to see how far you have progressed in your change by doing a little hunting."

"Uh, no. What are the other options?" I grimaced at the thought of killing something.

"We can go raid my fridge, but Mrs. Olsen has been gone for several days. We may not get lucky there. There's a Denny's across the river, I think. They're open twenty-four hours. What's your choice, my sweet?"

"Hmmm, such wonderful choices! Not."

Seventeen

We stepped into Denny's. I immediately noticed a familiar presence in the hopping restaurant. Friday night. Teens spilled out of booths and sat on laps at the tables.

I glanced around, trying to find the source of the familiar scent. Chance, already on it, pointed to the back of the restaurant for me.

In a booth furthest from the front door, two very familiar souls sat. My heart fluttered with excitement. I ran to the back of the restaurant. Jess bolted from the table. We embraced, standing in the middle of the restaurant for several seconds. Tears glazed my eyes.

Johnnie stood sheepishly behind Jess, looking at the ground uncomfortably.

"Hey there, Lora," he said.

"What the heck, Johnnie?" I grabbed him, giving him a hug, too. It felt great to see them both. "What are you guys doing here? Is this the hangout this year?" I almost laughed as I said it. Who would have thought it—hanging out at the Denny's. That's something Dani and her entourage would do. Just as I thought it, I saw it.

Dani, Rachael, Jason, and several other faces I didn't recognize sat at the table, staring at me. I looked at Jess and then laughed. She pressed her lips together in an exaggerated attempt to look offended.

Chance and I pulled two chairs up and joined Dani's entourage. The waitress ran over to take our order before I got to even look at the menu. Chance ordered us two rare cheeseburgers with fries and gave me a wink. Of course he knew what I wanted.

I turned to everyone at the table, smiling uncontrollably. "What's been happening lately? Anything cool?" I looked directly at Jess and Johnnie at this last point.

Everyone just stared at me.

"What?" I blurted and made eye contact with Jess.

"Uh, nothing, Lora. You look...uh...different, that's all. You look like... You're just not like yourself."

Johnnie piped in. "What's up with your eyes? They're all freaky colored?"

Oh crap. I forgot.

"They are rather freaky, aren't they?" Chance smirked.

I kicked him under the table. "So, yeah. Weird, huh? I guess my mom's eyes did the same thing when she was a teenager. Some disease where the color washes out of them."

"Is this surfer dude?" Jess asked in a monotone voice.

I nodded. "Oh, yeah. Sorry. Guys, this is Chance."

Everyone fake-grinned and said, "Hi."

"So anyway." Jess sipped her soda. "You look great, Lora. I just thought since you were so depressed or sick or whatever lately, you might actually look sick or something. Instead, you're glowing."

Johnnie nudged Jess with his arm and said, "Lora, it really is good to see that you're okay. I've been, well, we have been so worried about you."

"Thanks, Johnnie." I kicked him softly under the table. "What has everyone been up to? Anything new happening at school?"

"This is perfect timing!" Dani practically squealed. "The homecoming dance is next weekend. Now we all can go together! It's going to be so awesome. It's a formal so we can go shopping together this week."

Jess rolled her eyes. I almost laughed.

"Well, I don't know," I said.

Help! I screamed in my head to Chance. He had to have heard me, but he didn't help any. In fact, his amused half-smile tugged at his lips.

"This is actually the first time I have left the house in so long." I rolled a straw on the table under my finger. "I'll have to give it a few days to see how I do before I commit to anything. But, yeah, that does kind of sound like fun."

Jess gave me a sarcastic two-thumbs-up with a cheesy grin.

We ate and listened to Dani's gossip while getting in a few words on occasion for a while before everyone decided it was late, or early depending on the point of view, and time to go home.

As Jess and Johnnie walked up to the cashier, I got my chance to talk with them without everyone else around. "Hey, guys!" I said, glancing behind us to make sure Dani wasn't near. "If I'm not in bed all day tomorrow, do you want to hang out or something?"

"That would be great, Lora!" Johnnie seemed relieved.

"Yeah, give me a call tomorrow. I'll be home." Jess shrugged.

141

"Cool. It really was great to see you. I'll call you tomorrow." We hugged before Chance and I went out the door.

My heart felt like a rock in my chest. Fatigue showed his ugly head already. I probably wouldn't be calling my friends the next day, which made me feel worse.

Eighteen

Chance drove to his place. I was preoccupied with watching out the window at the passing scenery. Although it was night out, I saw everything zipping by as if it were in the daylight. My thoughts were on what Jess had said about my appearance.

"Am I glowing?" I asked Chance.

"Yes. You are the most beautiful creature I have ever seen." He kissed my ear before returning his gaze to the road.

Flutters filled my stomach. Beautiful, huh? I pulled the visor down and examined myself in the mirror. The brown in my eyes had reduced to tiny dots. Definitely not *my* eyes. And no longer me either. I didn't even recognize myself. Maybe my mom did have a disease of some kind that washed color out her eyes. It must have been hereditary and not any of this magic nonsense.

The car stopped, then Chance opened my door and pulled me out. Before I could take a breath, his lips were crushing mine in a passionate lock that sent electricity pulsing throughout my body. I felt paralyzed in his embrace.

Lora, my soul mate, my princess—how can you not know your beauty?

I returned his kiss with more force, parting his lips with my tongue to fill him with a fury of hot desire. He grabbed my hair and gently pulled while his lips traveled down my neck.

I needed to touch him, to feel his skin close to mine. I tugged at his shirt to pull it off, but instead it ripped, exposing his muscular chest and large biceps. I kissed every inch of exposed skin. Our breathing turned to panting. I pushed him with all my strength against the Jeep. He submitted and groaned. That sound drove me crazy.

My claw like fingers inched their way to the top button of his Levi's.

He grabbed my hand. *Not here.*

Now I groaned, but in disappointment. "I don't know what came over me."

He kissed the top of my head. "Mmmm. Whatever it was, I liked it."

His soft, moist lips gently brushed mine. I breathed in his breath and his scent, and I wanted to devour him slowly, but then exhaustion overwhelmed me.

He picked me up and carried me down the cobblestone boardwalk, into his house, up the stairs, and then set me on the couch, which he pushed over to the French doors onto the balcony. He wrapped me with the plush blanket and lay next to me, holding me close. His breath on my neck sent chills down my back. He squeezed me tighter and whispered in my ear, "The sun will be rising soon. Stay with me until then. It will be beautiful."

The early morning birds chirped in the trees below the balcony. They always knew when dawn approached. *Will I know what they know?*

"Yes," Chance said.

My eyelids felt like sandpaper. I struggled to keep them open. The sky faded into shades of violet and blue while stars dissolved.

Bird songs grew into a chorus of tweets, coos, and chirps, serenading the day to come. Golden light illuminated magnificent red and orange trees painting the mountains across the river.

Beautiful.

* * *

I awoke to river music teasing the rocky shore. My eyes opened to the brightness of day and focused on the beautiful man laying next to me—sleeping peacefully. White blankets rose and fell rhythmically to his heavy breathing. His flawless face emanated bliss.

He must have moved me onto the bed after I fell asleep that morning. A light breeze billowed the sheer drapes hanging on the open French doors and rays of sunlight peeked through.

I lay there motionless, studying his features as long as I could stand it without touching him. A small tuft of soft black hair hung from his forehead, gracefully curling over his eye. I gave into my desire and gently brushed it away. A smile stretched his lips before eyelids opened to reveal the humor in his crystal eyes.

"Good morning, my princess."

"Good morning." I cued back. "I'm sorry I woke you. You're just too irresistible." I leaned in to kiss his forehead then jumped up to dance around the room—energy pulsating through my veins. "What do you want to do today?"

Chance sat up. The blanket dropped, exposing his perfect, chiseled chest. He laughed when I had to pick my jaw off the floor.

"That's not a very nice thing to do!" I said.

He pushed out of bed and pulled a t-shirt over his glorious body. "Happy now?" He tackled me back onto the bed.

I laughed. "No."

He pinned me down and planted hundreds of kisses all over my face.

I squirmed to get him off me to no avail.

"Stop it," I said. Of course I didn't really want him to stop; it just felt like the natural thing to say.

He quit kissing me, but started tickling instead. *Oh no, you didn't!* Trapped. I couldn't move. My body thrashed violently underneath him and panic stabbed my guts. I couldn't breathe with him on top of me, confining me. Surges of energy convulsed throughout my body heightening all of my senses.

Chance leaped off and across the room.

Every single inch of my skin burned. It was happening. Muscles twinged and bones snapped. All that I had feared, the truth, the change, was real. And I couldn't stop it!

Nineteen

The pain only lasted a few seconds, not like I had thought. Standing on all fours in the middle of the room, I looked up at Chance who stared down at me. His eyes glazed with compassion and a small grin tugged the corners of his mouth. Feelings of wonderment and confusion ran through my mind.

All color in the room had turned to a paler version of the original. Like someone had painted with water colors instead of acrylics.

What was I?

Willing my body to move felt natural. I took long strides and leaped off the bed. Fawn colored fur covered my large cat-like feet. I had to find a mirror—fast.

"Follow me." Chance walked out of the bedroom into the bath where there stood a floor length mirror. I followed.

Why a cougar? I asked.

"Your animal spirit is chosen for you at birth. Although, you can choose to shift into any animal with your mind because of your heritage, only one animal is attached to your body. Your given animal must be cougar. Our bodies don't need to be told to shift into our chosen animal spirit."

A scared cougar stared back at me in the reflection. That was the first time I had ever been close to one, and I was closer than I'd never wanted to be.

Black lined my clear eyes, defining the shape that reminded me of a sideways teardrop. The flesh of my new triangular nose shined a soft shade of pink. Black fur covered two pointy ears while white fur spotted my chin. I turned several times to see the totality of my lean graceful body.

Moving on four legs felt natural. I crouched, stood on hind legs, rolled, leaped, and then finally walked out into the bedroom where Chance patiently waited. My movements felt graceful.

The concerned crease in Chance's forehead faded.

How do I turn back? I asked.

"You need to concentrate on the shape you want to take. Think about your human form—concentrate. Will your body. You need to desire it, to want it."

I thought hard, longing to have my two fleshy legs back. Before I realized that I had even begun to shift, it happened.

"That was so easy!" I said and stood, looking down at my naked body. I gasped, tried to cover myself with my human arms, and ran into the bathroom.

Chance stood outside the bathroom door just as I slammed it shut. "I'm going to put some clothes right next to the door."

"K—uh, thanks." Never, had I ever been completely naked in front of anyone in my life, until then. Not cool.

"Next time, when you concentrate on returning to human form, imagine yourself in clothes."

Now you tell me!

He laughed.

It took me a few minutes to compose myself—to get the courage to go back out in to the bedroom without being embarrassed. Just as I stepped out, Chance grabbed me. He embraced me tight.

"You don't ever have to feel embarrassed in front of me." He held me close to his chest. I fell limp in his arms, allowing all my anxiety about what just happened to disappear. Thinking about it, I laughed a little at myself—*I just turned into an animal but was more concerned about being seen naked! An animal! A cougar. Not human.*

How was that even possible? My brain hurt from thinking about it.

"We have a lot of planning to do now," Chance said. "Soon you'll need to take the journey with me to Theriania to meet your grandfather."

"But, today is not the day for that." I reminded him. "We told Jess and Johnnie we'd hang out." Excitement rose at the thought of seeing my friends again. It seemed like forever since I got to spend any time with them. They were probably devastated that I wasn't around. My thoughts drifted to the possibilities of what we could do that day. Hiking. A trip to Portland. The zoo! Ha. I would have fit in there.

Chance took a step back. "Lora, you've been asleep for several weeks this time. It is nearly the end of October."

All of my enthusiasm drained from me instantly. My legs wobbled. I sat down on the couch now in the room instead of the balcony. "Oh." Jess probably hated me for ditching her like that. "We can still call them to hang out can't we?"

"It's Thursday. They're probably in school. You should call tonight, if you want."

I sighed out loud and curled up on the couch.

149

I wasn't really looking forward to going to any of those fairytale lands. It was all too weird and scary. I didn't even know if I wanted to be a princess. I didn't know if I wanted to have all the shapeshifting abilities. What I *did* know was that I wanted to be with Chance. I wanted to spend time with my friends.

Chance sat at the other end of the couch. "There's no need for you to finish high school. The only reason why you are here is because your mother felt there was a threat to you in Theriania. There is no longer a threat to you. We need you there, my sweet."

"But why now? Why can't we wait a while longer? It won't hurt anything to wait will it?"

Chance was silent for a long time. I strained to listen to his thoughts. Nothing. His face was emotionless, smooth. He stared out the French doors.

"What are you thinking?" I asked.

"We should test your abilities. Tonight." He stood. "But for now, you must be starving. I'll get us some food." He ran out of the room. The iron spiral staircase clinked with footsteps and then stopped.

Alone. I longed to go to my secret spot—which by the way was no longer a secret, but still my favorite spot.

I stepped through the doors and onto the balcony. The cool, sunny air felt good, reminding me that it was late autumn. Leaves were sparse but still pretty on the trees across the river. The sun hung low in the sky. Morning.

Halloween was just around the corner. I'd definitely have the best costume. The most realistic animal costume ever.

I felt like a fairytale princess locked away in a tower with no escape.

You aren't locked away, my love, but yes, you are a princess. Chance stepped close behind me, pressing me against the railing with his warm body.

"Mrs. Olsen cooked ribs if you would like some. She'll be up with them in a moment."

"Perfect!" I turned around to return the embrace. "Now, back to my question of this morning. What would you like to do today?"

"You thought of Portland, didn't you?" he asked.

"Yes!" I love going to Portland. I love Seattle too, but Portland is my favorite. There is so much life, art, and energy there—it is a great place to people watch. "It's still early in the day. We could be there and back before Aubrey even gets home!" I heard the excitement in my own voice.

Chance glowed. "Then Portland it is! I had Dillon bring those clothes over." He pointed at the jeans and t-shirt I had on. "You can shower here if you want." His nose crinkled as if to say I stank.

"Who's Dillon?"

"You'll meet him tonight. Remember before you fell asleep last time, Julien went back to Takoda to bring back a couple guards? He brought my other two brothers, Dillon and Brian. They've been staying downstairs but are gone today."

After I had an opportunity to shower and eat, we took off for our adventurous day in Portland. It was only about a two hour drive at normal speeds, but Chance wasn't a normal speed driver.

151

Twenty

We sat sprawled out on the red brick steps of Portland's living room—Pioneer Courthouse Square—in the crisp air and watched people hustle from one place to another. Most of them didn't take the time to enjoy the beautiful weather. All types of people stepped on and off the light rail cars stopping periodically in front of the square.

A small musical group on one corner played rhythms on the bottom side of buckets. On another corner, a grungy looking old man played country songs on his acoustic guitar and people tossed coins in the hat sitting in front of him.

I stretched out on the step. The coolness of the brick seeped through my clothes. I closed my eyes and listened to the hum of the city. Car honking, brakes squealing, light rail doors dinging, people stepping, music, shouting…

After about an hour, we wandered to Waterfront Park along the Willamette River, tossing coins to the various artists and peddlers along the way. Crunchy leaves covered the sidewalks.

We bought chocolate ice cream cones and sat on the green grass overlooking the river and watched ships surge by. High speed traffic buzzed on the five bridges going in and out of the city.

Once my chocolate treat disappeared into the pit of my stomach, I laid my head on Chance's lap and closed my eyes. I imagined what my new home would be like. If what they told me was actually true. The pictures Chance had painted me were incomplete—he did say it was hard to put into words. I longed to see these fantastical lands. I had to have proof they existed. In my heart, I knew they did, but needed to see them. At the same time, I didn't want to leave my home in White Salmon. My heart bled at the thought of leaving Jess. And Johnnie, too.

I opened my eyes to find Chance's beautiful face above me. The sun shined all around him and through his dark hair. He winked while combing his fingers through my hair. This reminded me of when we officially met on the beach, when he lay next to me on my blanket. It was hard to believe it had only been a couple of months ago. I felt like we had known each other for all our lives—this beautiful creature and me.

He kissed my forehead.

"What are you thinking about?" I asked.

"About how life will be for us in the future." He looked toward the river and squinted from the sunlight.

"What do you think the future holds for us?"

He sat back, resting on his elbows. "Just as we discussed, but better. There will probably be a rough road ahead of us before we'll truly be happy, but the day will come when we'll all live without fear of Lord Xifan. You and I will live in a world of peace we'll have created."

I tried to imagine what he was talking about, but couldn't. There had never been a Lord Xifan or the terror he brought in my life.

I closed my eyes to rest. Magiclure sat on a fallen tree in a forest, fog all around him. He was in disarray. His once shiny black clothes were now torn and dirty, and his hair was matted with leaves poking from individual strands. His torn,

153

clear eyes stared right through me. No longer did they have the anger in them that I remembered. The fear I once felt rose in my throat anyway. I jumped to my feet.

"Did you see him?" I practically shouted at Chance.

Chance stood in full alert, scanning every direction. "See who?"

"Magiclure! Didn't you see him? He was broken, sitting on a log in the forest." I took a breath. "Weren't you listening to my thoughts?"

"Yeah, I was trying, but you weren't sending out a very loud signal. I didn't see him. Do you know what he wanted?" The skin on his forehead wrinkled.

"No. He freaked me out and I jumped up before he said anything."

"Come here." Chance beckoned me towards him as he sat back down. I curled up next to him on the grass. He wrapped both of his hands around mine. "Close your eyes again."

I stared at him for a moment—fearful.

"It's okay. I'm right here. I'll concentrate harder to hear your thoughts if he shows up again."

I lowered my head onto his strong shoulder, leaning my weight into him and closed my eyes. There was nothing at first, but then Magiclure appeared again, sulking in the same position as last time. His clear eyes met mine. They didn't seem as scary as before—almost kind. "Please don't fear me, Lora. I need to know where your mother is. Please help me help her."

"I don't know where she is. I've never even met her."

His expression dropped, hopeless.

"This is horrible news." He shook his head and gazed at the ground. "She's been searching for you. I thought she found you—"

"Where are you?" I asked.

"That's not important now. You need to leave White Salmon. It's not safe for you. Whatever you do, don't go to Ther—" His head jerked around. Out of the darkness, a bear leaped from behind and wrapped giant claws around him. He glanced back at me one more time—the fear in his eyes was unbearable for me to look at. He vanished.

My eyes shot open. "Did you see it this time?" I asked Chance.

"It was very hard, but I did get bits and pieces of him." Chance's brow creased. "Tell me everything he said again."

I went over the entire message from start to finish. He remained silent afterward.

"What happened to Magiclure?" I was almost afraid to ask, but had to know.

"I'm not sure." His voice came across gruff and annoyed. "We need to go. Now."

It was very difficult to stay at human speed as we walked back to the Jeep. The desire to run as fast as I could overcame me. Chance pulled on my arm often to keep me from walking too fast. We finally reached the Jeep.

"Where are we going?" I asked Chance who had not said a word since the park.

"Aubrey's first." His head turned straight ahead and the Jeep peeled out of the parking garage. I was pretty sure the trip home was going to be a quick one.

Twenty-one

A shiny black Jaguar—completely out of place in that neighborhood—sat next to Aubrey's powder blue Volvo in the driveway.

"Let me guess. Is that your brother's car?" I asked.

"Yeah, that's Brian's car. Let's be glad Dillon didn't drive." Chance snickered under his breath, but he still had an irritated edge to his voice. I wished I could hear his thoughts.

"What are you so worried about?" I asked. "This is supposed to be a fairytale, remember? Fairytales always have happy endings."

Chance hissed before getting out of the Jeep.

Our tiny house was full of beautiful men! I didn't think I'd ever seen so many hot guys in one room before.

Chance pinched my arm.

"Uh, ow."

"Brian, Dillon, this is Princess Loramendi of Theriania and Takoda." Chance gestured to me. They both stood from the couch and bowed in front of me. Blood rushed to my cheeks.

Brian took my hand to his lips and gazed up at me with clear blue eyes. "It is a pleasure to finally meet you, Princess." His dark hair, not as dark as Chance's, wisped around his face and was the same color as his long eyelashes. He wore a playful expression on his face.

Dillon, a mirror image of Brian, then pulled my other hand toward his lips.

"Twins!" I whispered. The room exploded in manly laughter. I pretty much wanted to hide under a bed.

Chance pulled me from his brothers. "Okay then. Now that you've met everyone, let's get busy." The twins sat back on the couch with smirks on their faces. So freaking cute.

Aubrey scooted over in her recliner to let me squish next to her. "It's been quiet around here without you, Lora. I've missed you." She squeezed my arm. It felt good to be next to her after so long.

"I think everyone is in agreement that we need to get Lora to Theriania," Chance said to the room. "The question is when?"

Julien spoke up. "Now. There is no reason for her to stay here any longer."

Aubrey put her arm around me. "Julien, you have to understand that this has been her home for almost eighteen years. This is all she knows. The only friends she has are here."

Yeah, so there. I pretzeled my arms across my chest.

"I'm aware of that." Julien clenched his jaw. "The fact is she's not safe here."

"Why is she unsafe? Because Magiclure said so? I know Magiclure. He would never hurt Lora but what he said doesn't make sense and until we get answers, I'm not putting my faith in what Magiclure says." Aubrey gave Julien her *look.* I knowingly grinned that there was no way Aubrey would let them take me. He didn't know her stubborn personality like I did.

Even so, I had to help the woman out. "I want to wait a little longer before going. I know you're concerned about my safety, but Chance is here and he'll protect me. I don't understand what the big hurry is all about. Theriania isn't going to be in any danger if we wait and I don't think that I'm in any danger either, do you Chance?"

"I'm not sure. Magiclure has no reason to warn us of danger, yet he went out of his way to do so." He looked at the shag carpet. "Let's give it a week. If there are any signs of danger within that week, we go to Theriania. Agreed?"

Everyone but Julien nodded their heads.

"Julien?"

"I don't agree with it, but I'll stay here to make sure everybody stays safe." Something about Julien told me he was loyal to his brother and now to me—to his family. He would never leave if danger was near.

I jumped up and ran over to Chance to give him a big hug. Then turned to Julien. "Thank you."

He nodded.

"I'm going to call Jess!" I ran into the kitchen, knowing perfectly well that walls weren't going to give me any privacy with this group. It just felt a bit more private I guess. The phone rang four times and then went to voice mail. My heart sank. I left her a message telling her I was better and wanted to hang out the next night or Saturday and to call me.

My enthusiasm was squashed with that phone call. My friends probably thought I abandoned them.

Chance walked into the kitchen and put his arms around me. "Let's go outside and test your skills." His voice was full of the excitement I lacked. My bottom lip went out into a little a pout.

"Come on. It'll be fun! I promise." He kissed my neck.

"Let's go!" I dragged Chance by the arm into the living room to say goodbye.

Julien followed us out the door.

The night barely clung to the warm air from the day. It could have slipped away and turned into a normal autumn night with a bite of frost. I zipped the front of my hoodie.

We walked down the street to the trail that led to my favorite spot.

"I don't know about this area," Julien said. "We should go further up the mountains for this. There may be people on this trail."

"I'll sense anyone getting too close," Chance said.

Instead of following the trail, we walked deep into the woods. It was difficult to maneuver around all the vegetation, but it was safer to be off the main path.

Once far enough from the trail, Chance stopped. "Let's test your abilities to choose different shapes. Start with a deer." He pulled me behind a tree. *Remember when you shift back to human form to think about the clothes.* He winked.

Like I needed reminding after what happened last time. "So, they'll just disappear when I shift out of them and reappear when I shift back into them?"

"Only if you will them to." He tapped his temple. "Remember to concentrate on what it is you want to shift into, like you did this morning when you turned back to human form."

I closed my eyes and thought about a deer. Bambi.

That won't work. Chances voice boomed in my thoughts. *A real deer. Not a cartoon.*

Okay. Jeesh. I remembered a white tail deer I saw munching on leaves at my favorite spot not long ago. She froze when she sensed me and then stared at me with large dark eyes. Her tail twitched before she galloped into the pit of the forest, no longer in sight.

Before I could think twice about concentration, I was on all fours.

My vision was a million times clearer in that form than in my human form. Edges of the fern bushes were jagged. Tiny bugs flashed through the air. Tree trunks jetted from the moss covered ground. Everything was a different shade of gray, except for the pale yellow trimming Chance's t-shirt.

I tripped over tiny stick legs and small hoofed toes. After a few minutes of practice, I leaped over a log, landing gracefully, and ran through the forest as fast as I could. Exhilarating.

Come back now. Chance thought.

I ran faster. The forest blurred at the edges of my vision. A large buck charged full steam behind me. Julien. I focused on the obstacle course ahead of me. Rock. Tree. Bush. And then a rushing creek. I stopped to listen to the babbling water and lap at the cold liquid. It quenched my parched mouth.

You're fast. Julien stepped next to me. Antlers stood tall on his head. *Let's turn back now, Princess.*

Bare trees surrounded the creek. *Are the trees dying? Look.*

The buck turned his head right and left, up and then down.

Dead vegetation dripped off broken branches. Ferns had turned crispy brown. Black leaves covered the forest floor.

A dozen brown, fuzzy spiders scurried up a tree trunk missing strips of bark.

Arachne! Julien leaped next to me and gently persuaded me to move along with his antlers. *We must go.*

What's Arachne? I ran through the forest the way we came next to Julien.

A race we don't want to bother. Let's leave it at that for now.

Whatever. I hated spiders anyway. No need to tell me twice to run away from them.

Chance leaned against a tree with sexy smeared all over his body. I could have kissed him, but Julien stood right there too.

I thought of my human form with clothes and suddenly became my normal self again.

"Let's work on your hearing skills. I'm going to think something without projecting my thought. You need to concentrate on listening. If you listen hard enough, you'll hear my thoughts. It may take time because you're still getting used to your new senses. Just listen." Chance sat on a rock, pulling me down next to him. Buck Julien walked away.

Forced listening was more difficult than I thought it would be. I heard the traffic zipping by from the highway on the bottom of the mountain and various snaps and cracks of the forest, but no voice from Chance.

Chance rubbed his thumb along my hand.

You can do this!

I jumped. "Was that you or me?"

"That was all you." He kissed my forehead. "You'll need to practice. It'll take time to control. Once you master it, I'll teach you to mute and project your thoughts."

"That's so awesome," I said. "Let's change into another animal now.

Julien stepped from the darkness of the forest in his human form. "We wanted to verify that you were able shift into multiple animals, and we proved that already. If you want to play, we need to go out further. We can do that tomorrow night if you would like."

"He's right." Chance stood and helped me up.

"Okay." I sighed.

Julien leaped in front of me, on the defense, squatting low to the ground.

Chance zipped next to him. A deep growl rumbled from his mouth.

I froze, not sure if this was a game or to be freaked out.

They guarded, staring into the trees.

I sniffed the air. Something had changed. A new scent was near. Fear mingled with a foul rotting odor. I looked from Chance to Julien, not sure what I should be doing.

Stay still, Lora. Keep your mind empty. Chance said.

Before I could comprehend Chance's words, Julien transformed into a giant brown bear. Ginormous paws held massive daggers for claws. He stood on his hind legs and bellowed a roar. Pointed teeth gleamed white in the ray of moonlight penetrating the forest canopy.

And then, he charged.

Twenty-two

The foul scent grew stronger.

Chance grabbed my arm and began to run. We ran as fast as cheetahs through the forest, only slowing when we hit the trail to a more human pace. We didn't stop until we reached the house where both Dillon and Brian paced like caged wolves.

"You stay here with Brian." Chance let go of my hand. He turned around to face his brothers. "Dillon, you come with me."

"I'm not stay—" They were gone before I could finish. Anger boiled in the pit of my stomach. They left me there with a babysitter no less!

"You're not the only one annoyed at the situation." Brian wrapped his arm around my shoulder and winked.

I pulled away.

He laughed. "Come on. Let's go inside." He held the screen door open. "Ladies first."

"Gee, thanks." I stomped into the house.

Aubrey wrung her hands at the kitchen table. I sat in front of her.

"Oh, thank God." All the tension melted from her body. "When the boys picked up Xifan's scent, I thought the worst."

"What? He's here?" I asked.

"I don't know. Dillon and Brian sensed him briefly and then nothing. What happened out there?"

"Julien freaked out and turned into a bear. Then Chance ran me home and told me to stay here. Lame. I should be out there helping!" I pushed my chair back.

Brian's foot stopped it. "I don't like this either, but we have to stay. If Xifan is out there, he might have an army with him and they'll take you. That would be bad."

"Well duh." I rolled my eyes. "But what if they kill your brothers? Don't you care about that?"

Brian chuckled. "My brothers can take care of themselves. Don't worry about that, Princess."

Aubrey stood. "Let's watch the news."

"Are you serious Aubrey? We need to go find out what is going on! I can't possibly sit here." I followed Aubrey into the living room. Brian stepped in front of the entrance.

"Oh my stars! Are you for real?"

"What?" Brian's eyebrows arched. "I know about your rebellious personality. I'm just taking a precautionary measure."

"Whatever." I flopped onto the couch.

"You can't possibly comprehend this. The Hornbroods will do anything to rule our lands and will take every opportunity to destroy you." The normal smirk on his face wasn't there anymore. His eyes were stern.

"Yeah, that's what I heard." I pulled my feet onto the couch and pushed a pillow under my head. The ten o'clock news flipped onto the TV. It made for good background noise while I concentrated.

I heard the neighbor's lab barking, the traffic flowing, a young couple arguing, children screeching, televisions, radios, cell phone conversations, and then I heard what I was looking for.

Three sets of footsteps on the street, heading this way. They were slow in their approach. I sensed that someone was hurt. I strained to listen to the thoughts of pain. Dillon. His leg bled, but wasn't broken. Everyone had small gashes and rips in their skin as well as their clothes.

I sprang off the couch and sprinted past Brian out the door.

Twenty-three

I raced to the end of the dark street, my footsteps only tiny pin pricks on the pavement—probably not even audible to the human ear. Brian was on my heels. Houses and parked cars sped by in a blur.

Chance held his arms open for me. I ran into them and squeezed his damp, hot body tight. He brushed away a few tears from my cheek I hadn't noticed.

With my new hearing skills, I gathered the entire fight from everyone's thoughts. It took a second to see the entire memory. A pack of Hornbrood scouts in wolf form had attacked my boys, but the Hornbroods were slaughtered by dagger-like bear claws and teeth and Takodian fighting skills.

Two wolves had bitten Dillon in the leg, but he quickly knocked the problems against a tree. Bones crushed and then the wolves whimpered on the ground before Dillon finally stomped on their heads.

I cringed and pulled away from Chance. "Why did they attack you?"

Chance glanced at his brothers and then at me. "They were after you, my sweet. Sent by Xifan."

My lungs spasmed.

Julien stepped forward. His broad shoulders were pushed back and his head held at an even stature, not high, but sure of his position. "We can't wait, Chance. We need to leave. Now."

Chance blew air from his mouth and raked fingers through his wavy hair. "Yeah, I know. Lora, I'm sorry. It's not safe here anymore."

My heart did the spasming that time. Those gorgeous boys put their lives on the line for me, protecting me, but I didn't want to listen to them. How could I leave my home to go to some strange land I'd never heard of where dangerous freaks roamed? How could I leave Jess, whom I missed already? I couldn't say a word, so instead I sank into myself and silently followed them all the way home.

Aubrey ran from the house when we stepped on the grass and demanded to know what happened. Julien filled her in.

"Hey, Dillon." I brushed his arm. "Thanks. Sorry you got hurt."

"Are you kidding? We need to be thanking you for the action!" Dillon laughed boisterously and pushed Brian.

Brian growled, but then his boyish smile returned. "I'm not babysitting next time. So not fair. In fact, I'm killing double what you got to kill tonight!"

"Next time?" I asked. "I hope there isn't a next time. If there is, I'm not staying out of it."

"There will definitely be a next time." Brian kicked Dillon's butt. "Just a matter of time."

"Really, Lora," Dillon said and then tackled Brian. "My leg will be healed up in a couple of days…just like new." Dillon winked at me from the ground and then put Brian in a choke hold.

Inside the house, everyone settled down into their own corners to rest. Chance locked the doors and bolted the windows before following me to my room.

168

"That's a pretty cool trick you got there," Chance said.

"What are you talking about?" I jumped onto the bed.

"How you tuned into what you wanted to hear. It was almost like you were sorting through our minds to gather what you wanted to know."

"Oh, yeah. That was pretty cool, but I was just doing what you told me to do. Concentrating."

"I wonder what your range is. We'll have to test it sometime." His expression turned serious and he looked at the wall. "You know what we have to discuss, don't you?"

"I know." I held onto the burning in my eyes.

Chance sat on the bed and I leaned against him. He stroked my hair.

"You should say goodbye to your friends tomorrow."

I pushed those thoughts out of my head. I didn't want to imagine Jess' face when I told her I was leaving. That she'd have to deal with the lameness of our small town all by herself. I was her only friend. Who would she confide in? Trust?

"Go to sleep now, Princess. I'll wake you early in the morning so we can catch them before they go to school."

Chance kissed my forehead, turned off the light, and left the room.

My pillow became a sponge. Silent tears turned to sobs. I couldn't bear the thought of telling them. I thought of not saying goodbye at all, just leaving, but that wouldn't feel right either. There was no way around it.

I wiped my face and thought of something less depressing. I didn't know how I ever breathed before I met Chance. As unreal as things were then, they seemed even

169

more so before he came into my life. Shifting, hearing thoughts, and strange faraway lands felt so natural.

I knew in my heart that I'd see Jess and Johnnie again. I had to. They were a part of me and I couldn't live without them.

The dark night soon turned to gray. I watched the sky out my window turn to day. The dreaded dawn had come—time to say goodbye to everything and everyone I had ever known.

Twenty-four

Once my stomach was empty and the heaves stopped, I peeled off the bathroom floor and crawled into the shower. I always got sick when stressed or scared or nervous. I was all of the above. Taking my time, knowing it would probably be my last in that shower, I let the hot water run over me to sooth some of my anxiety.

When done washing and brushing, I ventured out slowly to the living room and examined everything as if it were the first time I had seen it, but really the last. Old photos from my elementary school years hung in the hall. Cracks lined the plaster and paint. Dust powdered Aubrey's small doll collection on the shelf. When I was little I would spend hours just looking at things all around the house. It had been years since then and it felt like it.

"Hungry?" Chance's hug brought warmth to my empty heart.

"Nah, thanks." I crinkled my nose at the thought of food. My stomach rumbled but if I ate, it wouldn't stay down. "Let's go get this over with." I waved at the others sitting in the living room as I passed out the door.

We walked down the hill to Jess' house. The air held a slight chill that soaked through my wool sweater. School didn't start for another half hour and Jess should've been at home.

When we approached Jess' house, butterflies fluttered in my stomach. My guts turned sideways.

Chance rubbed my arm. *It'll be fine, Lora.*

As an afterthought, he said, "Wait a sec," and pulled a pair of dark sunglasses from his shirt pocket.

"Oh yeah. Duh. I bet they'd totally freak seeing my eyes so blue." I pushed the glasses over my nose to cover my new eyes.

Her car wasn't in the driveway. I hoped she was there, but relief toyed with my thoughts of having to say that word: goodbye.

I rang the door bell. No answer. "Well, we tried." I turned to leave, and then the door opened.

Mandy embraced me. "How are you?" She stepped back and pulled her robe tight around her front. "We've been so worried about you."

"I'm feeling much better now. Thanks." I fake grinned, not sure what else to say to her. "Is Jess home?" My voice trembled.

You're doing fine.

"No." Mandy glanced at Chance and back at me. "She went to the coast for the weekend with some friends. The school is closed for teacher conferences today. I'm so sorry."

"Oh." Now I knew for sure that my voice trembled. I gazed at the ground trying hard to hold in my tears.

Chance stuck his hand out. "I'm Chance. Lora speaks of you and Jess often. Do you know where Jess will be staying?"

Mandy was taken aback for a moment. "It's a pleasure to meet you." She shook his hand. "You know, you might actually be able to catch them. They only left about fifteen minutes ago. They had to pick up Johnnie and some others before getting gas in Bingen."

My heart skipped. "Really? Oh, thanks, Mandy!" We jogged up the driveway. "I'll see you later...thanks again!" I looked back at Mandy. I wouldn't see her anytime soon, but only hoped.

Mandy waved back to me. "Good luck, Lora!"

Once Mandy closed the door we ran as fast as we could at human speed up the hill. We jumped into Chance's Jeep. It only took a minute to get to the freckle of a town, Bingen.

"Wait Chance, pull over here." He stopped half a block away from the station. Jess' car was parked in front of the pump.

"Breathe," Chance said.

I took a deep breath in and closed my eyes. I listened like I'd never listened to Jess before. She pumped gas on the other side of the car. Something struck me as unfamiliar about her. She didn't seem like the Jess I knew and loved.

I opened my eyes. A girl about my age with dark, short hair came out of the market and walked behind Jess and threw her arm around her. Jess laughed, turning around to hug the girl. I had never seen the girl before.

Johnnie sat in the back seat of the car with someone— Rachael. I gasped. Rachael? I didn't believe it, but there they were sitting in the backseat of Jess' car giggling and flirting with each other. They both were happy. They *all* seemed happy!

My heart fell. I sat there for a few moments, watching, listening.

"Let's go," I said.

Chance nodded and leaned over to kiss me gently on the lips. He turned the Jeep around and drove off.

They didn't need me after all. I had no reason to stay. My eyes didn't burn, no tears washed through them, and only a small amount of loneliness pricked my heart. Not what I had expected.

I decided to just leave them a note and promised myself to come back as soon as all this chaos was over.

Dear Jess and Johnnie:

Aubrey's mother died and she needs to go take care of her father in Canada. Unfortunately, I have to go with her. I stopped by today to say goodbye but you had already left for the coast.

I am feeling much better. The doctor said I should be like new in no time—some weird virus, I guess.

I love you guys so much and will miss you. I will be back to visit soon.

Your friend always, Lora.

Twenty-five

The trip to Theriania would have been a nice lazy Sunday afternoon drive if not for the fact we were running from crazy shapeshifters who wanted to kill me and heading to an even crazier place. And today wasn't Sunday. The sun shined in and out from behind high fluffy clouds, casting rays of light through the giant trees onto the road. Lake Merwin sparkled a deep green-blue in the valley below us as we twisted and turned on the road through the mountains.

I wasn't sure if my nausea was from Chance speeding around the turns in the road or from the fact that we were now heading to a land full of fairytale creatures.

Brian had zero problems keeping up with Chance. In fact, I felt the energy of his impatience on several occasions as he wanted to pass us to go faster. Whenever Chance would start to speed up to appease Brian, Aubrey told him to slow down.

The fact that she had this power over Chance made my insides gooey. He respected her—he showed a respect for all his elders. A virtue I admired. She insisted on going on the trip, saying I shouldn't be traveling with four hormonal boys.

We slowed down when we entered into a dot of a town called Cougar. I'm not even sure you would call Cougar a town. There were a few buildings along a short piece of the highway and that was the entire town. I thought White Salmon was small, but Cougar had us beat for sure.

Just passed the last building, we turned down a single lane unmarked road.

"We're almost there." Chance squeezed my knee. It comforted me for only a second, and then my heart started racing again.

"I think I have to throw up," I whispered, looking out the window at the forest zipping by.

Glad she isn't riding with me! Brian's voice laughed in my mind.

Moaning, I leaned over to put my head between my legs. This seemed like a good idea at the time—I had seen people do it in the movies before—but it made my stomach spin faster. Chance jerked off the road.

My door opened and I was pulled out of the Jeep just as the contents of my stomach spilled into the ditch I stood in. Chance held my hair away from my face while rubbing my back as the heaves continued. Fluid burned out every hole in my face.

Completely mortified.

Aubrey handed me some tissues to clean my face and blow my nose. I waved to Brian and Dillon who waited in the car behind us and crawled back into the Jeep. They had stopped far enough away to not see the nasty scene I created.

"Okay. I feel better." I laughed a little. "My mouth would taste better though if any of you have some gum."

Chance leaned over to open the glove compartment where he pulled out a pack of gum to save the day. Julien held out a bottle of water for me too.

"Thanks."

"You're welcome, Princess. I'm glad you're feeling better," Chance said.

We passed several "No Trespassing" signs and one that read "Private Property." The further we went, the more signs there were. Finally, we came to concrete barriers blocking the middle of the road.

As soon as we stopped, Brian and Dillon were in front of the Jeep moving the concrete barriers for us to pass. Once on the other side, we pulled over to wait for them.

"Who owns this property?" I asked.

"The Therianians," Chance said. "The title of the property is inherited to the leader when leadership changes hands. Right now the title is in your grandfather, Lord Justus' name. When you take over, it will be put in your name. Each portal is owned by the leader of that land. Theriania owns about one-hundred acres here along the border of Gifford Pinchot National Forest. Occasionally, they'll get hunters or hikers trespassing, but the portal is so hidden and guarded with magic there rarely is a concern."

We drove for a mile further before stopping again. Brian and Dillon moved some shrubs off of what looked like a very well-hidden driveway. Once the camouflage was removed, Chance drove down the dirt road and sped up.

Anxiety began to build up again. Julien laughed in the backseat under his breath. Even Aubrey seemed amused.

Taking a deep breath, I tried desperately to control my nerves. Just when I thought they were under control, Chance accelerated again to nearly sixty miles per hour on the tiny dirt road.

Dead ahead, smack in the middle of the dirt road was a giant tree. The girth of the tree spanned the entire width of the road. There was no way around it. My ears pulsated to the rhythm of my heart. I looked to the backseat for some kind of consolation and only found Julien laughing. Aubrey gave me a reassuring wink, which didn't help much at all.

"Chance?" My voice was uneasy.

He looked over at me. "Calm down, Princess. I would never do anything to hurt you. This is the way to Theriania." He smiled all wicked like.

"That's not very nice!" I crossed my arms.

Brian and Dillon's laughter in the other car came to near hysterics.

Chance sped up even more, nearly going eighty. He turned up the stereo. Heavy metal guitars and drums filled the Jeep, vibrating the doors.

I covered my eyes so I wouldn't have to see the tree we were just about to smash into. I peeked through my fingertips—huge mistake. A scream worked its way out of my throat.

I braced myself and waited for impact. I held my breath. And waited some more. I gripped my seatbelt. My lungs burned, so I exhaled.

The Jeep slowed down. I opened my eyes to complete darkness. The headlights beamed a single stream of light ahead of us.

"Where are we? What happened to the tree?"

"The tree was an illusion," Chance said. "I'm sorry we scared you, but it's very rare we get to bring someone new into our world. And...well...I couldn't pass up having some fun." He laughed and reached for my hand. I pulled it away and punched his arm instead. "I guess I deserve that," he said.

"So are we there?" I asked.

"We are in a lava tube," Julien said. "At the end is where we'll leave our cars and enter the portal to Theriania."

I thought I'd probably have a heart attack before any of the Hornbroods could have their way with me. It became hard to breathe. "How long is this tube?" I squeaked.

"Not long. Breathe. Close your eyes." Aubrey leaned forward and put her arms on my shoulders from around the chair.

I tried to control my breathing, but confined areas had a way of messing with me. Chance set his hand back on my leg. Happy thoughts. The first time Chance and I met. Remembering him in the diner, how beautiful he was and how awkward I was—this made me laugh out loud. Chance laughed too.

The car slowed to a crawl. I opened my eyes. It was no longer pitch black. Huge lights hung from the ceiling, illuminating the cave and hundreds of cars parked along the walls, like we arrived at the mall. Chance found an opening for the Jeep and parked it there. Everyone jumped out except me.

I listened to the muffled silence of the deep cave—deep beneath the Earth's surface—trying to get a grip. *Is it far from here?* I thought to Chance.

The portal is just over here, my sweet. He gently drew me out of the Jeep.

The dry air was cold. Steam billowed from our nose and mouths. Water dripped and seeped from the top of the cave and down the sides onto the ground.

I grabbed my one duffel bag of clothes. While packing, I had tried to stay optimistic that I would be going back to White Salmon soon and only needed one bag. Besides, I didn't know what they wore in Theriania. In my imagination, they wore beautiful clothes made of fine silks. My cotton tees, wool sweaters, and jeans were a far cry from my imagination.

"We'll get this later." Chance tossed my bag into the Jeep.

"Come, Princess Loramendi, come see your home." Dillon put his warm hand on my shoulder and led me toward the back of the cave. Chance walked on the other side of me while everyone followed until we got to a wall. I looked up at Chance in confusion.

"Patience, Princess." Chance moved to the wall and gestured for me to follow him. A hidden pocket in the rock held a square piece of glass. He pressed his hand against the glass, holding it there for a few seconds and then pulled his hand out. He stepped back. I followed.

The wall suddenly became transparent. Light shined through, illuminating the entire cave and glowing off the sparkling walls. I held my hand to my forehead to block the brilliant light so I could see. I squinted and my eyes adjusted, and I saw Theriania for the very first time.

Twenty-six

A gasp escaped my lips. Before us was exactly what Chance said it would be—hard to put into words. Light blazed from the green grass, the sky, the trees, the glass-like buildings, everything.

We stepped through the wall. There was no visible sun in the sky. There was just a colorless brightness above us, but intense color burst from everything else.

We stood on the greenest grass I had ever seen. That's a pretty tall order coming from someone who lived in Washington. In fact, I wasn't sure I had ever seen that shade of green before. Millions of vibrant white daisies grew on the hill. I wanted to log roll down the hillside, then run through the daisies.

Everyone laughed, most likely hearing my thoughts. Dillon and Brian crouched to the ground into the position.

"Ready, set, go!" Brian yelled. They both rolled and laughed the entire way down. Once they reached the bottom, they tackled each other, playfully punching one another.

We were standing at the edge of a forest overlooking a city with tall glass buildings reflecting sparkling light at us. The hills before the city were speckled with smaller glass and metal buildings.

Chance stepped behind me, putting his arms around me. His warm touch brought a flush of blood to my face. I turned my head up to kiss his neck and he bent to return my kiss.

Before his lips touched mine, he was gone, ripped from me, almost knocking me over. Aubrey jumped to my side and held onto my arm to steady me.

Brian and Dillon bolted up the hill effortlessly—like lightning.

Julien crouched in the center and slightly in front of the other three boys in front of me. Chance's voice hissed in my head. *Something's not right. Keep your mind closed. Don't let anyone know who we are. Follow my lead.*

Just as he gave the commands, several wolves with clear blue eyes appeared in front of us. I counted maybe ten. They were bigger than any wolf I had ever seen or imagined. To the sides of us, about twenty small green creatures appeared. Ugly and slimy, they had big sharp teeth that protruded from their bottom jaw. They too had piercing blue eyes.

The only thing I could concentrate on was the order Chance gave us to keep our minds closed. I tried my best to think of nothing. That didn't give me any time to freak out about what was happening, otherwise, I'm sure I would have wet my pants.

The wolf in front of the pack shifted into a huge man with shiny black armor covering his body. "Welcome to Theriania." His gruff voice was not very welcoming. "What is the purpose of your visit today?"

"We are here to pay our respects to Lord Justus and to see if he has heard word about his daughter yet." Chance's voice was strong and loud, not a voice I had heard from him before. "We are sent by the royal family of Takoda." He sounded far more powerful than the giant man in front of us.

"We shall escort you, then." The man turned back into a wolf.

Several of the pack moved behind us as the wolves in front walked toward the city. Chance motioned for us to follow. His face was stone cold as were the other boys' expressions. Aubrey didn't hold any expression.

The small green creatures scurried next to us and closed in on the sides. They made little snorting and grunting sounds and worked twice as hard to move at the rate we were walking because their legs were so short. Their bodies looked like the blobs of slime we made once in grade school.

It occurred to me that we could be moving at a much faster rate. I wondered why we were walking at a human pace. Chance looked back at me, reminding me to stop wondering. My mind went blank.

We traveled through a small village of shiny short buildings where various life forms walked the narrow streets. Funny magical creatures of all shapes and sizes, exotic animals, even a few flying creatures that looked like fairies from story books, were going about their day in the little village.

No one on the streets looked at us. I wished I could know what they thought of us walking with guards, why they wouldn't take notice of us. Chance glanced back at me. Quickly, I abolished that from my mind too.

The scent of meat, all kinds of yummilicious flesh, from fried to sautéed, hit me from the small outdoor market we passed. My mouth watered at the aroma. I hadn't eaten all day.

We finally arrived at a giant building made of glass and crystal. It actually glowed.

The stained glass doors contrasted the white light with vibrant colored panes. Shades of red, blue, gold, and green radiated from the doors that slowly opened as we approached, following the wolves into the palace.

We entered into an open room with thick walls that seemed like ice. A crystal chandelier hung above a massive staircase that wrapped halfway around the room. Sitting on the various pieces of white furniture were creatures in human form talking amongst each other, peacefully.

A fireplace roared on the left of the room. The walls on that side were covered from floor to ceiling with books. Giant-like people, elf-like creatures, and even a couple of those slimy blobs lounged in front of the fire, reading. Long, dark hallways extended off the main room.

The head wolf turned back into the giant man form. "Wait here." He headed down one of the dark halls to the right of us.

Chance turned to me, gripping my hand while looking directly into my eyes. For a split second, I saw the love in his eyes and felt it in his touch—it quickly turned cold and blank again.

Remember what I said. His voice was in my mind.

I nodded just as the giant man came back into the room.

"Come with me." He ordered us again. We followed, but the rest of the guards stayed behind.

He led us down a long and dark hallway. The only light came from the dim glow of the checkerboard flooring and from the door at the very end. The closer we got to the door, the brighter the white light became. When we entered, all darkness shimmered away.

A speck of a man with white hair sat in front of a wall length window. Without turning to look at us, he lifted his arm and motioned us to come to him. The giant wolf-man bowed and walked backward to exit the room. We inched our way forward.

The small man turned his chair to face us. Immediately, everyone bowed to the ground. Except for me, but then I did as they did, bowing at my waist toward the ground. I looked at Aubrey to see exactly how she did it, not knowing the proper way to bow to royal people, or creatures in that case. I mimicked her curtsey.

"You may rise," the small man said. He looked from Chance to Aubrey and then to me, holding my gaze.

Chance cleared his throat. "Thank you for seeing us, your lordship. We have come from Takoda to find that you are well." Chance bowed his head. "Tell us, Lord Justus, is there word of your daughter or your granddaughter?"

I had to bite my tongue not to laugh at how goofy he sounded. And then I realized what he had said. Lord Justus. My grandfather.

Lord Justus snapped his attention from me to Chance. Sagging aged skin on his face crinkled around his eyes. "What would you have of them?" His voice cracked.

"Please forgive me for the inquiry, your lordship. We meant no harm. We only mean to know so that Takoda and Theriania will unite in peace with the marriage of your granddaughter to our prince." Chance's confidence astounded me and it was more than a little weird to hear him talking about himself in the third person.

"Ah, yes. This would interest you, wouldn't it?"

"Of course, your lordship. Would it not interest you to live in peace without fear of Lord Xifan?"

The old man raised his brows. "Is this what you do? You fear Lord Xifan?"

"Do you not?" Chance asked. Tension was building in the room. Although I was doing my part by blocking my mind, I felt hostile energy emanating off everyone around me.

"Yes, our alliance would be a strong one. I do have to agree. But, what would I do about the alliance between Theriania and Hornbrood, dear Prince?" A deranged psychotic sound curdled from deep in the old man's throat, almost like a laughing hyena.

"You would never have made a pact with Hornbrood, Lord. You would never do that to your people or your family." Chance's words spewed out of his mouth laced with daggers.

A low grumbling came from the old man and turned into a wicked laugh that echoed through the entire glass room. "They left me here to rot!! They have not returned as she promised me!" Spit flew out of his mouth. Veins bulged from the thin skin across his forehead. "It is my choice to make an alliance with the one person who has been here for me, dear Prince." His eyes began to glow.

"What if we found your granddaughter? What if we could bring her to you right now? She could take this entire burden off your hands." Although Chance's voice was still sharp, the volume had dropped a few notches.

"It is too late. She is dead to me. The pact has been made." His laugh rolled through the room.

I couldn't hold my thoughts anymore. I choked from the fear mixed with anger. Chance looked back at me, his eyes warning.

"*This* is the man that is supposed to be my grandfather? He is supposed to save me from those evil Hornbroods? This

186

crazy old man?" My fists clenched and my bones began to crackle. I struggled to hold myself together.

The old man's eyes grew wide. "I knew there was something about you." It was no longer his voice, but darker and deeper than before. He growled and glared at me. The old man fell back, exhausted, into his chair.

Chance jerked around as fast as light. *Go!*

All of us ran after him as he pushed his way down the dark hall and changed into a giant grizzly bear. I hadn't witnessed him do that before, but pushed the vision out of my head. There was no time for emotions. Julien, Brian, and Dillon followed Chance's lead and snapped into running bears, too.

Aubrey stayed close to me as we ran. The bears surrounded us, knocking the small green blob creatures against the glass walls. They splattered into green slime.

Wolves leaped from nowhere, but never once penetrated the barrier of bears around us. We continued to run at warp speed. The power of the bears was like a force field crushing everything that came at us. We shattered through the stained glass doors and zipped through the villages. The attackers never stopped.

My heart felt like it was going to burst into my ears from pounding so hard. The fear that we'd never get out of that awful place was overwhelming.

Don't doubt us!

Something swooped down from the sky. Aubrey pushed me forward and the creature missed me by inches. "What was that?" I screamed, looking up, horrified at the dragon flying above us. "I'm losing my friggin mind!" I shouted at the top of my lungs.

187

Just when the dragon began to swoop down, it happened. I'm not sure how it happened. I didn't plan it. I shifted into a stronger and bigger dragon, then took off into the air!

I soared high above the smaller dragon, feeling the air against my face—the exhilaration was unbelievable. A small insane laughter came to my mind when my claws dug directly into the smaller dragon's back, ripping gashes into its scaly skin. Its body weakened and I flung it across the sky into the mountain side. I glided over to where it hit and found the injured dragon heaped on the ground.

I felt his pain; his cries pierced my mind.

I will spare your life, little dragon. I swooped down and turned back to human form to stand vulnerable next to the dragon. I gathered rubbery leaves from beneath a strange tree and pressed them against the dragon's wounds to stop the green ooze trailing down its body.

No need, my lord. The dragon chuckled. *But, thank you. You have a kind heart.*

I pulled the leaves away. The scales quickly knitted themselves back together, leaving a trace of a small scar which vanished before my eyes.

"Whoa."

The dragon rose slowly and then bowed before me. *Thank you, my true lord. I will tell our people you have finally returned and that you are good.* He stretched his wings and took off into the air.

I nodded before turning into my dragon form to fly back to the others. When I landed, I shifted into a bear to help out my protectors. I tossed Aubrey onto my back and ran along Chance's side, feeling his energy—his pride.

Power surged through my bear body. I had never had so much strength in my life. With a simple bat of my giant paws, wolves went staggering to the ground. It was starting to get fun hitting wolves out of our way as we ran to the portal. They whimpered and fell over like bowling pins.

Chance shifted to his human form. He opened the portal and we charged through. It changed to stone once we reached the other side.

"Others will come after us soon. We must hurry!" Chance hollered. We hopped into the vehicles and took off into the dark cave.

Twenty-seven

Our vehicles raced through the cave at nearly seventy miles per hour. Gray light poured into the opening of the tunnel and Chance floored the gas pedal just before we reached it. We flew out onto the dirt road and into night air. I could finally breathe.

"Where are we going?" I asked.

"Takoda. It's the only safe place." He shot a warm glance at me. "Your grandfather seems to have gone mad and no doubt will send his soldiers after us."

"Ya think?" It just figured. I never had a grandfather before and now that I had one, he was totally psycho. That, and a shapeshifter.

I shifted my gaze out the window and tried to absorb everything I couldn't think about in Theriania. It was so real while we were there, but thinking on all the weird creatures I had seen a few minutes prior seemed like literature, totally fiction.

My grandfather, Lord Justus, couldn't have always been that weak and small. The anger of losing his daughter must have boiled his brains or something. If only I could talk to him and find out about my mother, what she was like, where she may be, and how I could find her. He had to know something I didn't.

Pity for my grandfather weighed on my heart. He had been alone for over seventeen years with no family. I vowed to go back to him as soon as things calmed down.

Jess would never believe any of this. If I hadn't been the one to turn into a flying, scaly lizard, I wouldn't have believed it either. It was like my whole being had been awakened from a slumber. I knew exactly what to do and when to do it. Flying through the air was exhilarating, but for some reason, didn't feel like a new experience.

I didn't fear this Lord Xifan that so many feared. He was nothing to me other than an evil dude who broke up my family. Evil always loses in fairytales.

When I shifted in Theriania, all reason was thrown out the window and when our lives were threatened, a newfound power pumped through my veins. A strength and fearlessness I had never felt. Before today I would have cringed at seeing so much blood at my hand, but now, it felt empowering to crush the lives of those attacking us. The power of change— the power to become something stronger and fiercer than I had ever imagined was just a thought away. Fear was abolished in an instant when I flew above that dragon, flinging him into the mountain. But even more importantly, when I forgave the dragon a little of my old self came back. With forgiveness and compassion we gained a supporter. That dragon will no doubt come to our aid if we ever needed it. I was confident.

The urgency to get to Takoda became apparent to me. No longer did I question my abilities or new skills. In order to save my grandfather and possibly my mother, we had to defeat Lord Xifan and his followers. There was no other way.

Chance must have been listening to my thoughts. A strong sense of pride and a sexy strength emanated from his body. His foot grew heavier on the gas pedal, his grip tighter on the steering wheel. He watched the road ahead of us, but I could tell he was smiling.

You are a true leader, my princess, my sweet love. The future is clearer to me now than ever. You have brought that clarity; you will bring that peace.

Brian and Dillon raced next to us and in my mind I heard everyone's howling cheers. And then laughter from all, including myself.

Twenty-eight

The laughter had subsided but the energy still lingered when we pulled into Portland International Airport's long term parking lot. Heavy rain clogged the windshield and glare from the street lights made it difficult to see in the dark lot.

We grabbed our bags and caught the shuttle bus to the terminal.

A wave of panic came over me when we approached the counter. Aubrey tapped my shoulder with something. My passport. "Thanks, Aubrey!" I said with relief.

Although I had never been out of the country, let alone out of the Pacific Northwest, Aubrey decided it would be a good idea for me to get a passport last spring. I had thought, at the time, she was going to surprise me with a trip. Even though she told me it was only because it was good to have, I hoped she would take me somewhere exotic for the summer. But that never happened.

I wasn't sure what to stress out more about: the fact I was a princess of a fairytale land, my boyfriend was a prince from another fairytale land, I could turn into all sorts of animals including dragons, evil fairytale creatures wanted to kill me, the grandfather I never knew turned out to be psychotic, I was going to meet Chance's parents soon, or my new concern—flying in an airplane for the very first time. My stress meter was about to explode.

Chance nuzzled against me. "You want to talk about it?" His breath warmed my ear. He could whisper in my ear forever and I'd be happy.

"I can't even remember now," I whispered. All my worries disappeared whenever Chance touched me. He wrapped me in an embrace.

"I can't breathe, Chance." I tapped his arm.

"Oh, sorry!" He laughed, releasing me.

We didn't have to wait long for a flight. One left for New York within an hour. I had wanted to go to New York City my entire life. We only had a two hour layover, but I hoped to at least see the city out the window. I couldn't wait.

When we finally passed all the security checks, Brian and Dillon spoke at the same time, "I'm starving!"

"Great idea, I'm starving, too." I followed them into a café next to a gift shop.

They seated us near a window with a view of the runway. It was fascinating to watch the airplanes take off and land—like a synchronized performance.

I must have been completely enthralled with watching the airplanes because before I knew it, a big platter of steaming hot cooked flesh was presented before me.

I ordered for you, Princess. You were enjoying yourself too much to interrupt you.

Thanks. I sawed into the bloody mess, not considering anyone around me, and shoveled a piece into my mouth. Savory, chewy goodness melted on my tongue.

"I know I taught you better manners than that, Lora." Aubrey gave me the look.

"I'm sorry. Yes, you did." I sat up straight and spread a napkin on my lap.

Brian and Dillon smirked at me. If Aubrey wasn't in hearing distance, they probably would have said, "Neener neener neener."

I rolled my eyes. "What? Jeesh!"

With fifteen minutes until we were able to board the plane, I walked through the shops lining the terminal. Chance followed.

I bought gum and a couple of paperbacks to read on the plane. I was pretty sure I would be done reading them before New York and would need to pick up a couple more before the next leg of the trip.

I went to the bathroom about a million times at the airport and didn't drink any water. I had heard that the toilets on planes were in tiny closets with no room for moving. I freaked out just thinking about using them.

We finally boarded the plane. The cabin smelled of stale air. I took a deep breath and blew it out. We didn't have to go far because Chance had bought us first class tickets. Nice.

"How else do you expect royalty to travel?" Chance asked.

"On a private jet." I gave him a cheesy grin and fluttered my eye lashes.

"That would be nice," he said.

***

The plane descended into New York. I closed the novel I was almost finished with. The on-flight movie was one I had already seen so it was a good thing I bought the two books.

The captain announced we should be able to see the Statue of Liberty out the windows if we were interested. My window flap had been open the entire flight so that I wouldn't miss anything. Although I only saw clouds, blue

195

sky, and sun, I often gazed out of it when feeling too confined.

There she was. No amount of television shows or pictures in books could have prepared me for seeing the Statue of Liberty live. I couldn't believe we were so close. The clear sky allowed for a perfect view. I measured her with my index finger and thumb. A good inch in height.

I so wished we could stay for just a short while to see all there was to see—Broadway, Times Square, Grand Central Station...

"We'll come back my sweet," Chance whispered in my ear. He pulled my hand to his chest. *We'll travel anywhere your heart desires.*

We weren't waiting long in the New York airport before we boarded the next plane for our final destination—Moscow.

By far the best thing about first-class was the chairs. They reclined just right, allowing me to lie back and fall asleep for the remainder of the trip. It felt like forever since I had slept. Chance made for a perfect pillow.

"It's time to wake up, my beautiful princess."

I stretched in the chair, yawning and rubbing sleep out of my eyes. I leaned over to rest my heavy head back on Chance's shoulder. It couldn't be time to get up already, I thought, it hadn't been long enough. He was so comfortable and warm when I snuggled up next to him, I didn't want to move.

"You need to wake up. We'll be landing in just a few minutes."

The plane bounced onto the ground, jerking me awake and off of Chance. "Dang it!"

Everyone stood and grabbed their things from the overhead bins.

When the doors finally opened, it was a race to see who could cram themselves into the aisle to get off the plane first. I won of course.

We stepped into a foreign world. Not only did everyone look and speak different, they thought in their own language. I listened to the thoughts of a woman sitting in the waiting area. I couldn't understand her.

All the signs were written in Russian words. I had to rely on listening to Aubrey's thoughts after she read a sign and translated it in her mind. Apparently, she knew the language. Yet another bit of info withheld from me my entire life. After a few attempts of that, I figured it was just easier to follow everyone else and not worry about where we were going.

We ended up at a counter with pictures of cars all over the brochures and keys hanging on the wall behind the counter.

None of the boys were very pleased at all with the mini-van we got. It was the most logical choice as there were six of us.

Brian quickly corrected me. "Actually, Lora, it is not a great choice because we will be driving through some rough rugged areas to get to our destination. We may be better off getting two vehicles that have 4-wheel drive."

Chance agreed. Apparently, the only vehicles they had with 4-wheel drive were new Hummers because they got two of them—one was a bright yellow and the other was black.

"Now that's what I'm talking about!" Dillon said and climbed into the driver's seat of the yellow one.

Aubrey looked over at me with a grin on her face and rolled her eyes.

"The seats are heated!" I pushed the button on the console to start warming up our comfy leather seats. I spent a good ten minutes playing with all the gadgets, including the stereo, on the console until we pulled out from the underground garage. My interest was instantly averted to the outside.

My thoughts immediately went to the images in my head from books and television of what Moscow should look like. In my mind I had pictured only medieval type buildings with the funny soft serve ice cream tops like the buildings of Red Square or of the Kremlin.

It looked nothing like what I thought it should look like. The exterior of the airport was very modern as well as the buildings around the airport. I also had the silly notion that it snowed constantly in Moscow. Right now, there was only a thin layer of snow on the ground. Not the mounds of snowy hills always in movies.

"Are we going to get to go through the city?" I kept my eyes glued on the window.

"Unfortunately, this isn't a sightseeing trip. I promise we'll come back another time." Chance half-grinned, seeming amused.

My mood changed from excitement to dread. My stomach twisted and turned again as I took a deep breath to fight back the anxiety from everything that had happened the past couple of months. I watched a train speeding by on the tracks running along the highway and tried to block my thoughts so no one would know the sadness creeping over me.

A small girl watched out one of the windows of the train—I waved but she must not have seen me.

I wished that I could still be home in White Salmon, living a normal life with my friends Jess and Johnnie, going to school every day and working at the diner on weekends. I wondered if they even missed me at all, or had they long forgotten about me. They seemed so happy the last time I saw them, like I never even existed. I didn't even get to meet Jess' new friend.

Tears pooled in my eyes, but I was able to hold onto them. Nobody seemed to notice. I finally found a way to be alone after all. Just close my thoughts.

Although both Chance and Aubrey were with me, I still felt lonely. Kept in the dark for my entire life, how could I possibly be able to succeed at what they expected of me? To lead a fight against Lord Xifan? I had never been in a fight, not even on the playground at school.

I leaned my head against the cold window. Dark mountains hovered over the vast empty meadows sprinkled with the snow. The train was long gone.

Twenty-nine

It took nearly thirty-two hours to finally get to a town called Inta. Julien and Chance took turns driving our car while Aubrey and I slept most of the way. Brian and Dillon also swapped out drivers just as much as we did.

We made several stops in towns along the way for supplies. There wasn't a lot of traffic through those parts I gathered from Aubrey's mind after she spoke with a store clerk. The people of the towns were very friendly.

Inta was the end of the line for our Hummers. We turned onto a small dirt road and slid along for about a mile. The deep snow forced Chance to turn on the 4-wheel drive. The forest was thick on both sides of the road. If Chance hadn't turned, I never would have seen the road.

We came to a small brick shack in desperate need of some repairs. Chance turned off the engine.

Brian pulled next to us, then jumped out of their Hummer, stretching his arms into the air. "I didn't think we would ever get here! That drive takes longer and longer every time. I like Lora's idea. Next time, we invest in a jet!"

"I'll pitch in for that, my brother!" Dillon slapped Brian with a high-five.

"What do we do now?" I felt so out of place and totally unaware of what was going on. The problem with all of us being pure-bloods was that everyone blocked their minds. I couldn't hear anything from anyone, except for Aubrey. But she didn't have any answers as she had only been to Theriania.

"We will rest and freshen up here for a little bit. I'll make a fire," Chance said.

Brian and Dillon ran for the shack, charging through the front door.

"Once we are rested we can head to the mountain by foot. There are no roads that we can take."

"By foot?" I asked. "Is it close?"

Chance raked his fingers through his hair. "It's a good hike that'll take us a few hours in human form. We can shift, but one of us will have to carry Aubrey. That may be the way we go to save time."

From looking at the exterior of the shack, I was expecting the inside to be just as shabby, but was pleasantly surprised to find just the opposite.

Brian and Dillon had already spread themselves out on two plush couches with fuzzy throw blankets in the living room.

A kitchen with dark granite counter tops and dark finished cabinets with stainless steel appliances sat in the back portion of the shack. The bedrooms were hidden underground, down a spiral staircase. Two of them had massive four-post beds covered in pillows and fluffy blankets while the third held a computer, a TV, and a small couch in the corner.

Aubrey brought in a grocery bag full of food she had bought at the last stop and Julien trekked outside to an outbuilding in the back, carrying a gas can to turn on the generator.

Once we had our fill of food, everyone relaxed in their own area of the house. Chance and I went downstairs to sleep on one of the big beds. Aubrey gave both of us *her look*. Knowing full well what *her look* was for, I pulled her aside in embarrassment.

"Aubrey! It's not like we are going to do anything. Chill out!" I practically screamed in a whispered tone.

"I'm just warning you, that's all. Nothing better happen. It is their law that you remain a virgin until you are crowned ruler of Theriania and Takoda." Aubrey stated with an agitated tone equaling my hushed voice.

"What? What if I'm not a virgin now?"

"You are." Aubrey's confidence irritated me.

I stomped to our room, and then tiptoed in front of the door, which let out a rusty scream and foiled my plan to startle Chance.

"You don't really think you were going to scare me, do you?" he asked, his brows raised.

"I would have if the stupid door didn't squeak." I ran into the room and leaped onto the giant bed with a somersault. Chance tackled me, pinning me down to the bed. I lay there, pretending to be helpless while I laughed. "Just don't tickle me."

"What are you going to do if I do?" He teased.

"Please don't." I pleaded, not wanting to expend the energy needed to squirm away from him.

"Well, okay, since you said please and are so dang irresistible." He leaned over and kissed me and twirled my hair with his fingers. I exhaled and allowed the tingling to move from my lips down my entire body. He pulled away, putting his head on the pillow next to mine. His arm rested over me.

I turned to face him, questions plaguing my mind, but closing it to him at this moment. I searched his face, his mind, for my answers. But he had his thoughts closed as well.

"What's bothering you, my princess?" His voice was smooth and low.

"Well," I held my head up, chin in hand, "what exactly should I expect when we arrive in Takoda?"

He closed his eyes.

"Hey! Aren't you going to answer me?"

"Listen, Princess."

Closing my eyes, my mind was flooded with images of a beautiful kingdom. In a plaza in front of a stone palace, thousands of creatures gathered in various forms—human, animals, fairies, even those ugly little green blobs that were in Theriania. Hundreds of creatures flew in the sky and dove into the celebration.

Everyone danced to music like no other music I had heard before. Wind instruments with a modern twist created a joyful sound.

When I opened my eyes I found Chance beaming at me. "What do you think?"

"It's beautiful, but," I bit my lip, "that's not what I was asking." I sat up and cleared my throat. "What is going to be expected of *me*? How can I become a leader in a matter of minutes? A few weeks ago, I was just a plain girl from a small town going to high school. Now I'm not even human. I'm a princess of two lands about to go to war. I know nothing about war. I know nothing about being a princess or a leader of any kind."

His stare was too intense for me. I looked away, toward the wall with its many imperfections. "Why were they celebrating?"

Chance sat up. He gently pulled my face away from the wall to look directly at his beautiful, hypnotizing eyes. "They were celebrating because we found you, the princess who will unite us and bring peace. That's exactly why you were born! It's in your genes to be great, no matter how you were raised. It doesn't matter that you have never fought. You don't have to learn it; you know it." He held my hands. "Do you remember when we discovered that you were changed? You simply turned into a cougar without having to think about it."

"Yeah."

"Or how in Theriania you simply turned into a powerful dragon, once again, without thinking about it?"

I nodded.

"Don't you see? You didn't have to be taught, it came naturally. Your breeding, sorry about the term, has insured that you are the purest blood there has ever been. Pure Therianian as well as pure Takodian. Everything you ever will need to know will come to you. Your instincts will be all you need."

What he said made sense, but I was still unsure about it all. I wished we had more time.

"I'll always be at your side. You'll probably get so sick of me and tell me to leave. But, I won't." He shrugged. "So, stop worrying about it and get some rest." He kissed my head. I snuggled close to him.

There was no way I was going to stop worrying about it. I decided to take everything as it came to me and to rely on my instincts. It felt better knowing Chance would always be at my side in case my so called instincts didn't kick in. I dreaded what would come the next day.

***

The sky had dumped more snow while we slept. The Hummers were buried in giant mounds of the white stuff. Aubrey had set out a snow suit and boots for me that she found in one of the walk-in-closets. Amazingly, they fit perfect. I humored her by wearing them even though I wouldn't need them.

Julien led the way into the forest. It was difficult to walk through the snow but became easier the deeper into the forest we went. The trees held most of the burden on their branches. Once far enough there was no possibility of being seen, we shifted.

We traveled as a pack of wolves. Aubrey rode on Julien's back at the head of the group. Dillon and Brian played like puppies, tackling each other in the snow.

I was fascinated how warm the fur all over my body kept me. I had often thought about that in the past, wondering how the animals stayed alive in extremely cold weather. It just didn't seem like a layer of hair could be that protective, but I was mistaken. I wished I could pet myself to feel how soft my fur was. I bet it was soft, it looked pretty soft.

Would you stop it already? Brian's head snapped around. *Yes, your fur is soft.*

Sorry 'bout that. I made a mental note to block my thoughts when thinking important thoughts like the texture of fur.

Chance nudged me playfully. I ran ahead of Julien, making sure snow flew off my heels at Brian. Chance followed me.

"Hey! That's not very nice." Aubrey complained when snow hit her, too.

I yelped an apology.

Chance tackled me, pushing me through a snowy drift. I growled and then laughed at how funny it sounded.

Chance howled. From behind us the other wolves in our pack howled as well. I decided to join in, not sure exactly what the howling was all about. I stretched my neck back, letting my vocal chords ring.

"Owwww ow owww wooooo!"

If there were any people out in this forest, I'm sure they would have been running for civilization at hearing our menacing howls. This lasted for a few minutes before we began trotting toward our destination again. Chance and I led the pack and the others weren't too far behind.

It's not far now, my sweet.

Wonderful! There was a little too much unintended sarcasm in my thought.

It'll be fine. Just breathe.

Our footsteps crunched in the snow. Occasionally, a clump of snow fell from the trees. Other than that, the forest was silent.

Chance, is it Halloween today? I asked.

Yes, it is.

Oh, man. No one is going to see my perfect costume.

The Halloween prior we all went to a party Dani held at her house up in the hills. I wondered if they were going to go there tonight. I could picture Johnnie dancing with Rachael while Jess danced with her new friend. I was sure they wouldn't have any time to think about me and remember all the good times we had in the past.

I sighed and my head hung to look at my furry paws.

Chance rubbed against me again.

Stop! Julien's voice rang in my head.

Chance froze and then strained his neck to look behind us. His clear blue wolf eyes widened for a second before transforming into an angry glare. The skin on his muzzle crinkled to expose dagger white teeth.

I searched his thoughts, but he had blocked his mind.

The hair on his back stood straight up and he crouched a little lower to the ground, readying to pounce. A growl gurgled from deep within his throat.

Fear gripped me, not allowing me to move. I held my breath and forced myself to slowly turn around.

Do not fear, my love. Take a breath and follow your instincts. Chance's words appeared in my thoughts.

I pushed my body to face forward.

A man dressed in black stood before us. Dark wolves and slimy green blobs surrounded him, their clear eyes burning holes through us.

My breathing stopped again. I sucked air in and then forced it out. In and out.

"Princess Loramendi," a thick gargled voice said out loud for all to hear. The voice came from the man—if one could call him that—that stood directly in front of us. "We have been waiting for you for so long, your grandfather especially." The voice held sarcasm in it. When he spoke, jagged teeth covered in black goo pointed out of his bottom jaw. A near translucent layer of skin sagged from his thin face.

He reminded me of the scared young boy that I had dreamt about. He had cried about voices and pain, and his father had no sympathy for him and transformed into an angry bear.

I had no clue what I was supposed to say to this creepy dude standing in front of me with a bunch of green slimy creatures surrounding him, telling me he has been waiting for me.

Lord Xifan. You know you are not allowed here. What business do you have here? Chance hissed—his wolf body tensed with anger.

Wolves and green blobs surrounded us. They inched closer. Instead of scaring me, it really irritated me.

"Oh, but Prince Chance, we are only here to pay our respects to you and your newly found betrothed." Black gunk seeped from the corner of Lord Xifan's mouth. He held his pale hand with long boney fingers up to wipe it. "We mean no harm." He stated with a certain amount of amusement.

That whole scene seemed as farce as a fairytale to me. Xifan the man reminded me too much of Xifan the boy. I shifted into my human form. I wore the ivory dress from my dreams. It flowed behind me, dragging in the snow when I approached him. Chance followed me, shifting into his human self, dressed in an ivory suit. *Nice touch*, I thought.

"Lord Xifan, it is a pleasure to finally meet you." I must have been going with the flow because I didn't know how I was able to say that without my voice being cracked and high pitched. Trusting my instincts. "I have heard so much about you." It was my turn to have the humorous tone.

Lord Xifan bowed his head slightly. "You are as beautiful as your mother, Princess. She will be so pleased."

"Do you know my mother? Have you seen her recently?"

"Yes, I see her daily. I will let her know that you asked of her."

A twinge of anger snapped my heart, but it was easily controlled. "How, may I ask, have you become fortunate enough for my mother to grace you with her presence on a daily basis?"

"Oh, yes. I was so hoping you would ask! You see, your mother, she lives in Hornbrood now. As my guest." A wicked laugh bellowed from his disgusting mouth.

If I wasn't upset about my mother I probably would have laughed at how ridiculous he sounded. "I see. Perhaps she's ready to come home now. She has been gone so long." I directed my fierce gaze into his clear eyes, trying to penetrate his thoughts. No luck. His thoughts were locked in a fortress.

"I enjoy her company. She chooses to stay." He spit the words out as if he had bitten into a sour apple.

"Is that so? And what if I come get her?"

"Yes, please do. I would love your company as well!" He giggled insanely and clapped his hands.

Chance let out a hiss and lunged forward. I grabbed his hand and pulled him back.

"What are your plans, Xifan? My grandfather claims you visit him, too. Don't you have your own family?"

"Don't flatter yourself so much," he said.

I took a step closer and with a steady voice said, "You may have my mother and perhaps my grandfather, but there is a little flaw in whatever plan you are concocting in that evil head of yours You don't have me! You will never have me."

Xifan laughed again. "You have no clue, do you?"

His dark wolves were only feet away.

"Of course you don't." He shook his head. "You will be running to me soon. And when you do, you'll beg—"

A deadly cry of growls and barking echoed from somewhere in the forest. It bounced off trees. Adrenaline charged through my limbs.

Xifan's face crumbled into a painful grimace, the same pain I saw on his face as a child. "No!" He looked left and then right. "Run!" He disappeared in a plume of fog.

A few wolves and green blobs scurried to get away into the trees. Larger wolves crouched down and growled at us.

"Great! Does this mean I'm going to have to get this really pretty dress dirty?" I asked. The horrified look on Chance's face at my comment almost made me laugh.

"You do realize there are about a hundred or more Hornbroods surrounding us that want to kill you, don't you?"

"Yeah, thanks for reminding me!" I shouted out sarcastically.

The creatures closed in, building a circle around us. My claustrophobia kicked in with sporadic breaths. I tried to control it. Just went with the flow.

Chance shifted into a giant grizzly bear, and he knocked away one Hornbrood at a time, tossing them into the air. The Hornbroods continued closing in, slowly, crouching to the ground in the same stance I just saw Chance in when he was a wolf. The hair on their backs stood straight up while they snarled, showing their sharp white teeth.

210

Snow fell in light fluffy flakes and landed softly onto the forest floor. I concentrated on the sound and slowed my breathing.

In an instant it happened. I wasn't thinking, just breathing. I heard it before he even had an opportunity to react to his thoughts. One of the wolves hunkering close to me had decided to leap at me, to tear my face off. Time slowed for that short moment.

Excitement built inside at the anticipation for him to do it; I was actually looking forward to it! "Come on, little Hornbrood! Try it!" I smirked down at him. As he lunged forward, my body cracked and stretched into the giant dragon once again.

I turned and my tail swiped him off his feet along with several others standing next to him. My tail then dropped on top of him, crushing the creature beneath the weight.

The Hornbroods slowly backed away, still low to the ground and growling, into the trees. Chance looked over to me in his bear form with blood splattered all over his fur.

I shifted into human form. *It can't be over, can it? Where are they going?*

"It's not over." Chance stood next to me in his human form.

I couldn't see or hear the rest of our group. My mind searched the forest for them. Horror filled my heart at the thought that they had been killed.

I ran to where they were before this all began, Chance close behind me. Only Hornbroods were there, scattered, lifeless, on the ground and in the trees. *How could this be?*

Chance searched next to me, never leaving my side. "They can't be far." His confidence surprised me.

We followed bear tracks leading away from the gory scene where we last saw them. They split about a mile away from where we started into three different directions. One set had human tracks next to them—*Aubrey.* We followed those.

Soon the bear tracks turned into another set of human tracks. As our speed increased, the trees became streaks of blurry white and brown out of the corners of my eyes. We continued in silence as thoughts plagued my mind—horrible thoughts of what could have happened—that I had to force away in order to continue.

"Why did the tracks split?" I asked.

"I'm not sure. Maybe they felt like they were being followed."

Help! A scream shook my thoughts. I froze, trying to find the source within my mind. I listened harder, concentrated. Finally, Julien. He was backed up against a stone wall, trapped, with Hornbrood wolves closing in on him.

"Hurry!" I said.

We took off as fast as we could.

I listened while we ran. Julien swatted at the Hornbroods, one by one. It occurred to me just then that the Hornbroods must not be that smart—instead of all of them jumping on him, they attacked a couple at a time.

Where was Aubrey? I listened, but I couldn't hear her.

The muscles in my legs burned. I couldn't go any faster.

We approached an opening in the forest and in an instant both Chance and I shifted. We ran out of the forest, colliding with the Hornbroods. My massive dragon body was so strong that I could take out five to ten Hornbroods at a time. Their defenseless bodies cracked as I flung them through the forest.

A sharp pain ripped into my back. I jerked around. A Hornbrood in cougar form dangled from my tough skin by his teeth.

I swung my arm around and ripped him from my scales. Flesh tore away. Pain flashed from the site.

I was about to smash the small cougar in my bare claw. I stopped. His thoughts were filled with fear and pleading not to die. His clear eyes held despair and pain.

I listened to all of the Hornbroods surrounding us. Their eyes were no longer fierce like I thought they were. They didn't want to hurt us. And they didn't want to be hurt.

Gently, I put the cougar down onto the ground. *Please don't crush me.*

Fear not little cougar. I will not harm you.

I shifted to human form and sent a thought to the others to not harm any more Hornbroods.

Chance and Julien turned toward me with confused expressions.

"Hornbroods, hear me now!" The voice speaking was mine, but I didn't recognize it. "We will not harm you. Please, stop attacking us and you will be set free." Everyone stopped and gazed at me.

I caught a glimpse of one of the Hornbrood's thoughts, a bear, standing near me. His family was being held in a prison, hooked up to machines. How typical, I thought. Lord Xifan must have forced these creatures to fight by threatening their family. The bud of hatred I held for Xifan bloomed.

Chance read into the same thing. He nodded with understanding. "Do not fear for your families. We will shelter you in Takoda. We will soon conquer the evil lord

213

and you will be free to live peacefully once again." Chance's voice echoed throughout the forest.

Chance's words didn't bring any joy to the Hornbroods. They must have endured a lot and couldn't feel happiness. One by one they turned into their sad human forms of skin and bones. My heart broke for their misery. I thought of all the weak Hornbroods that I had already killed. How could I have been so blind?

Chance's and Julien's faces fell. Sadness overwhelmed me at the death we had brought to so many innocent creatures. Souls obviously controlled by Lord Xifan. This so-called lord was really starting to piss me off.

Aubrey! Where is Aubrey? I looked feverishly around the forest

Chance and Julien began frantically searching as well.

Help me! I finally heard her thoughts and I ran to find her. Hundreds of feet trampled behind me.

The land ended. But her thoughts were so loud there. I jumped from the ledge, through fluffy clouds, down a cliff that seemed to have no end. I shifted into my dragon form, soaring through the clouds until I reached the source of my concern—Aubrey.

To my horror, I found her hanging from a tree growing from the side of the cliff in the mist of the clouds. I nudged her onto my back and flew to the top.

Flying out of the clouds, a wall of clear eyes set in pale faces greeted me from the ledge.

Everyone backed away to make an open space in the snow for me to place Aubrey. Once she was safely on the ground, I turned to my human form, hovering over her. Chance squeezed in to take a look.

"I think my leg's broken," she mumbled.

Chance looked at Aubrey's leg. "We can carry her to Takoda."

Brian and Dillon showed up. From what I gathered from their minds, Julien had already filled them in on the events. They had all split up early on to deter anyone from following them. Little did they know, the group was actually waiting for them. Julien and Aubrey had walked right into them.

"Let's go!" I said, excited to leave that dreadful place.

Julien picked up Aubrey and we all walked in human form to the portal of Takoda giving my excitement plenty of time to turn into dread.

Thirty

"We're nearly there!" Chance grabbed me from behind and held me close, causing mild convulsions to run through my body. He had to have known by then that his touch started my blood racing.

I turned toward him. "Thanks for keeping your sanity when I've pretty much lost mine."

"Are you serious? If it weren't for your brains, we'd still be slaughtering the Hornbroods. Besides, if that was losing your sanity, you need to lose it more often. Royals are always insane anyway." He laughed.

Great. I didn't look forward to living with insane shapeshifters like my grandfather. He had to be kidding.

We stopped at a dead-end. Well, I guessed if we were mountain climbers it wouldn't be a dead-end. But, since we weren't climbing the mountain that day, it was a dead-end.

Chance cut through the icy snow bank against a rock wall rising into the sky. He dragged his hand along the jagged surface and then held it in one spot against the rock for several seconds. He walked to a giant fir tree next to the wall and caressed the bark, chanting something in a language I couldn't understand.

The wall began to shift. A small avalanche of snow fell at our feet. Then the wall opened completely, without a sound.

Chance locked his arm through mine, and we entered the opening in the mountain.

Welcome to your home, my sweet, where you will be cherished by all!

I wasn't sure if I wanted to laugh or cry or runaway. Definitely insane.

Instead of stepping in through a forest like we did in Theriania, we were in a village next to a giant stone castle; the kind I imagined in fairytales. The sun shined a yellow orange glow that lit up the world with cheer. The air smelled of wild roses, and birds sang in the trees around the castle.

Once we were completely through the portal and the stone wall closed, horns announced our arrival. I stood very still and watched the world come to life. Therianthropes gathered around us and above us in windows and walkways. Rose petals fell from the sky. Therianthropes cheered and sang. The love overwhelmed me. Tears welled in my eyes. Chance squeezed my hand, his energy bringing me strength to continue with the madness.

Creatures of all shapes gathered in the streets, waving, singing, and cheering as we walked down the cobblestone street to the giant castle in front of us. The heavy wooden gates opened. Two centaurs stood on the walkway above the gates playing giant horns, welcoming us into the castle.

Once we entered into the castle, the horn players stopped playing. Taking their place were the most angelic voices I had ever heard. A small choir to the side of us sang a melody of peace. Chills rose over my entire body.

I looked behind me to see if everyone was with us still— Dillon, Brian, and Julien holding Aubrey were all there. Each of them bowed their head. Aubrey waved.

Therianthropes in fine silk clothes lining against the walls bowed when we passed them. Ahead of us, a man and a woman sat in two high-back chairs of gold at the top of wide spiraling stairs. They stood when we came to the bottom of the stairs.

Chance led me into a deep bow almost down to the ground. My head spun, but Chance held me steady.

The angelic singing stopped.

"Welcome to your home, Princess Loramendi." The woman's voice was as smooth as Chance's. In a blink, she stood at the bottom of the stairs, pulling Chance and I up from our bowed stances.

"Mother." Chance embraced the delicate woman and she kissed him on the cheek. She glanced at the brothers behind us and nodded. They stepped forward to kiss her hand, one by one.

The man somehow stood at the bottom of the stairs now too, joining in on the family reunion. He looked like an older version of Julien and Chance, tall and strong. He then grasped my hands, kissing them and looking at me with clear eyes. He guided Chance and I to the top of the stairs that overlooked the interior of the castle as well as the village outside the walls.

He drew breath. "Takoda welcomes home her future, Chance and Loramendi! The future leaders of all therianthropes around the world. They will unite us and bring a peace to our kind we have not seen for many years! God bless Chance and Loramendi!"

The entire village erupted with cheers. Streamers and confetti dropped from the sky. A cheerful melody full of happy notes played on wind instruments bounced off the stone walls. It was the same music I heard in Chance's vision. Thousands of therianthropes in human form sang and danced below in the village.

The sun, far off in the distance, slipped further behind the mountains, reminding me of the sunsets at home. At that moment, I realized this was my home. These were my people. My therianthropes. They counted on me to bring peace to their world, this beautiful world.

Anger seared my heart as I remembered Lord Xifan—his arrogance. Everything about him repulsed me. I wanted to crush him so he could no longer bring fear and pain to so many.

I looked up at Chance who gazed at me. His half-smile appeared. He leaned down to kiss me gently. I thought I heard fireworks.

He slowly pulled away. A half-grin grew on my own lips and I raised an eyebrow. I could play that trick, too.

I am Princess Loramendi, the future leader of therianthropes. The future destroyer of Lord Xifan.

**watch for
the next installment of Lords of Shifters
Coming Soon**

Special Thanks

A number of great peeps helped Loramendi's Story become what it is today.

I'd like to thank my first readers, Katie McAllister and Breanna Kurth. Katie has read four different versions. The original was titled Dreaded Dawn. Breanna suggested that Chance is stiff competition for Edward Cullen. I suggested that Breanna is totally rad.

PDX Word Wranglers, Gary Corbin, Monique Bucheger, Randal Houle, and Terry DeHart all had a hand at hacking away some parts of this story. Thanks to all of these excellent critique groups and partners.

Thanks to the awesome DarkSide Publishing authors for helping edit the final version of Loramendi's Story and all the cool stuff they spew. A special thanks to Megg Jensen, Karly Kirkpatrick, and GP Ching.

I'm thankful for a group of people who heard my call for beta readers and responded. Valerie Burleigh, Tony Graff, Stacey Wallace Benefiel, and Rebecca McAllister deserve big hugs for their most generous help.

Of course, my family deserves a shout out, too, for putting up with me and my writer ways.

And a huge thanks to you, the reader, and to book bloggers and reviewers who help spread the words.

About the Author

Angela Carlie writes fiction about young people. She lives in the beautiful Pacific Northwest with her husband and son. She loves reading, writing, hiking, kayaking, and traveling.

For more information, please visit www.angelacarlie.com or www.angelacarlie.blogspot.com

She loves hearing from fans, so please feel free to send her a message on the above sites.

Enjoy this sample of

Dream Smashers
By Angela Carlie

Now Available

ONE

Friday, October 2nd

Hope, wrapped around my wrist in the form of hemp and beads, created by the innocent hands of my mother as a kid—a dream smasher in the making. Frayed and worn, it reminds me that my mother hasn't always been how she is, and lets me believe that maybe she could someday be a real mom. That thought ranks high on the totally-never-going-to-happen scale, but one can still have hope. Besides, she did a wicked job at making it, so it's a pretty cool accessory. I haven't taken it off since I found it stuffed in a junk drawer in her old room.

"Autumn." Grams' phlegm-heavy voice snaps me out of my thoughts. "Eat your breakfast."

Jeannie, a lifelong waitress who escapes her husband every morning by going to work, slides a plate of eggs and hash browns under my nose. According to the whispers from the lips of old ladies, Jeannie sometimes works double shifts to avoid going home.

It's funny the things you notice that you never noticed before when secrets touch your ears. Like a bruise on an arm that could have come from running into a wall, but now seems more than a simple accident, or a subtle limp that wouldn't have been given a second thought, but now weighs heavy on the heart.

The aroma of breakfast stirs the monster in my stomach. "Thanks, Jeannie."

She winks at me and walks away.

Grams turns back to her conversation with her two lady friends, one a retired high school teacher, the other a widowed hair dresser. Smoke billows from Grams' cigarette, creating thick smog around the group, and she slurps a cup of coffee while they chat about the latest gossip. I never understand how they have so much to talk about. We eat breakfast here every single day, and every day they have at least thirty minutes of chatter to spill.

It's a typical Friday in the town of Cultus, Washington, which is nestled like a nasty tick into the armpit of the state. With a population of thirty-five thousand, it's not a small town, yet there is absolutely nothing to do here. Well, nothing that won't get you into trouble or destroy your life. There's a reason why this town has a high crime rate and is known for its access to methamphetamine.

The bell on the door jingles, and my best friend, Rainy, walks through. She waves her hand in front of her face and coughs. "Dude, you're gonna die of secondhand smoke and crap."

Tell me about it. I don't smoke, yet I'm pretty sure nicotine seeps from my pores.

Rainy stops at the amber glass to check her bleach blond mullet—ratted on top and long in the back—in the faint reflection before flopping down next to my grandma on the green vinyl bench. She grabs the cigarette from Grams' hand and smashes it into the ashtray. Grams is too enthralled with her conversation to notice.

"You really shouldn't eat with them if," Rainy raises her voice, "all they're gonna do is smoke like chimney stacks." She turns back to me. "Aren't you even gonna ask why I'm early?"

"What time is it? I didn't notice it was early." Actually, she's probably right on time, instead of late as usual. "And why do you look so nice? Why are you wearing a skirt?"

Rainy never wears skirts, but today she sports a plaid hot pink and neon green schoolgirl skirt, complete with a matching petticoat. The skirt may be new but her standard t-shirt and Converse are the same. She says the eighties look makes her stand out in the crowd. Not that she needs big hair and retro clothes to stand out.

"I have a date after school," she says. "And so do you."

"What?"

Grams' selective hearing must have zapped her because she snaps her attention to Rainy.

"Yeah. Remember that website I was telling you about?" Rainy pauses as if I should know what she's talking about. "You know, the one where lots of kids hang out in chat rooms and talk art crap and stuff?"

"No. You never told me, because I would've remembered that." Rainy talks to a lot of people, unlike me, and thinks she tells me things when she really told someone else. She won't admit to it, but it's a problem that emerges on a regular basis.

"Yes I did. Whatever, it doesn't matter. The point is, we have dates and they're from the chat room." She grabs a piece of toast from my plate and spreads jam on it.

"What do you mean, we? I don't know anybody from this chat room, so it looks like you're on your own."

"I set you up." Her teeth crunch into the toast.

Grams thin lips twitch from their ordinary frowning position into a straight line, her effort at a smile. "Do your parents know about this date?" she asks Rainy.

"Of course, Grams. Chaaa." Rainy rolls her eyes.

Grams nods her head in thought. Her two friends lean toward us, a little more interested in our conversation—like this may be the best gossip of the day. News flash: Rainy forces Autumn to go on a date. Better yet, Autumn agrees to go on a blind date! But that's not going to happen, so they may as well find something else to whisper about.

"Sorry, I'm not doing that again," I say to Rainy. "Last time you totally ditched me with that freakazoid at the movies...remember?"

"Come on. He wasn't a freak." Rainy grins. "You were just mad that I got the cuter guy, that's all." She throws the crust from the toast onto the plate then reaches for my water. "It will be different this time. I saw a picture and he's hot. Real hot."

"I don't care. I'm not going—I've got stuff to do." Well, I wish I had stuff to do.

Rainy scrunches her face in disbelief. "Like what? What could you possibly have to do on a Friday night?" She sighs. "I'm your only friend, dork. Remember?"

"For your information, I have plenty to do and it's none of your business."

Grams hacks up a wad of phlegm and spits it into a napkin—totally embarrassing me, as usual. Not that there is anyone here to be embarrassed in front of. Rainy's already familiar with Grams' smoking habits. The old ladies whom Grams hangs out with smoke just as heavily as she does. Thus, every morning is a chorus of hacking old ladies. The run-down Matt's Café is regularly filled with other hackers of the geriatric nature.

"You know you don't have anything better to do," Grams says. Her friends nod in agreement. "What are the boys' names?" Grams points an unlit cigarette at Rainy.

"Evan and Caleb." Rainy shrugs and lifts an eyebrow toward my direction.

"Their last names?"

"Laverne, I think. They're cousins. Why?"

The three old ladies banter at each other. "Evan's Delores' son." "She volunteers at the Senior Center." "Good church-going folk." "They'll be safe."

Rainy lets out an exaggerated sigh. I kick her under the table.

"Go out with Rainy and have some fun." Grams gives me her serious look. "If you don't, I'll have you polishing my spoons all weekend."

My grandma is famous for collecting antique silver spoons. She fills drawers and racks and cupboards and boxes in storage full of the shiny pieces of metal. She is a member of the American Spoon Club and gets spoons through mail order. She travels to antique stores once a month in search of odd spoons or to find what she perceives as exciting spoons.

"Each spoon has a history," she once told me. She owns a spoon rumored to have been Hitler's and one from Abraham Lincoln. She even found some freaky weird spoons that don't look like spoons at all from, like, ancient times or something.

The last time she forced me to polish spoons was six years ago for stealing candy from the supermarket.

Rainy's eyes light up. She points at me. "Ha! You don't really want to polish spoooooons, do you?"

"Gee, thanks, Grams."

"And when you're done with the spoons, you can come to church with me on Sunday. You're sixteen, sweetheart. Take it from me…"

Oh, here we go.

"…you need to loosen up a little and enjoy some good clean fun. You need to go out tonight with Rainy. You also really should start coming with me to church because there are some nice kids there you can make friends with and join the teen church group after school."

I roll my eyes.

Her finger slices through the air toward me. "I mean it, Autumn." She lights another cigarette and blows blue air out of her nostrils. "You spend too much time at home worrying. You don't have to worry about the world, or about me, and you especially don't have to worry about being like your mother."

That did it. I stand and grab my book bag. "We need to go."

"You're not going to turn into her by going out once in a while. Don't run away every time I bring her up."

"I'm not running away, we just have to go to school." Lie. I'm not really in the mood to talk about my so-called mother. I jerk my head toward Rainy and she gets up.

"Fine, but just know that you are not your mother. You're nothing like her."

Yeah, you said that. "I know Grams." I bend down to kiss her peach-fuzz cheek. "Don't spend all day here. Get home and take a nap or something."

Dear Lord, please watch over and protect Grams while I'm away. Keep her safe.

I march through the door, not looking back to see if Rainy is following. Once I get to the end of the block, Rainy's footsteps on wet pavement and heavy breathing catch up with me.

"Would you slow down?"

"We're going to be late." I turn to wait for her. "Do you even want to go today?"

She steps next to me, out of breath. "Not really."

"I only want to show up for art class. Do you want to hang with me in the art room while I finish up an assignment or do you have better things to do?"

"Nah, I'll hang. So, what do you wanna do 'til then?" She walks double-time to keep up with me. Her short legs can never keep up with my long ones. "Do you wanna go to the falls? Or, how 'bout the pot-holes?"

I sigh. "Not really. Let's just go to the pit."

"Cool."

The pit is an abandoned one bedroom house we lay claim to on a regular basis, just a few blocks from school property. It's the sort of place that Grams would vomit hot chili peppers over if she knew we hung out there: dark, creepy, broken. But what she doesn't know won't hurt her. Or me for that matter.

We sneak around back and enter through the sliding glass door.

I sit on a wooden chair that we found broken in the back last month. There had been three of them we rescued, just dumped like garbage. It wasn't difficult to restore them. A little wood glue, some sandpaper and paint, and now we have chairs representing all the primary colors.

The blue chair is mine today, to express my mood. Rainy sits in the red, as usual.

"Come here a sec," Rainy says. "I wanna show you our hot dates for tonight." She pulls out her laptop from her bag.

"What's the big deal about these dates? You know I'm drawing here, don't you?" I hold up my sketch pad. "He better be Taylor Lautner gorgeous."

The laptop beeps, waking from its slumber.

"What are you drawing now?"

"Just an assignment for school." I toss my sketch pad to her.

She looks at it for a moment. "Who's this?"

"It's, uh, Jacinda." My mom.

"Really?" She stretches pink gum from her mouth and twirls it around her finger. "I thought it was you for a minute, but it looks a little different. Is this what she used to look like?"

"Yeah. I found a picture in one of Grams' albums."

"Wow. She used to be pretty."

"Yeah, she *used to be*." I don't remember her being pretty though.

The last time I saw her she was a walking skeleton with skin. She didn't look like that picture at all. Her black hair, no longer thick and full, had become thin and stringy, like doll hair. The dirt caked under her yellow finger nails turned the tips of her fingers black, and the rash on her face turned her skin red. Her teeth no longer resembled the pearls she inherited, but rather nuggets of coal she dug from a mine. Those that weren't missing.

They called Jacinda a miracle child because the doctors told Grams she couldn't have babies. Grams got pregnant with her at thirty-five—almost old enough to be a grandma rather than a first-time mom.

"How's your brother doing?" I ask.

"James?" Rainy shrugs. "He's gained weight and hasn't run away from rehab in over a month. He gets out next week."

"That's good, isn't it?"

"I guess. I don't think he'll stay clean when they let him out. Once a tweaker, always a tweaker." Rainy flips through the pad. "Wouldn't it be cool if gravity didn't work for meth addicts and they all floated out into space? They should totally build a colony for them on the moon so we don't have to deal with them."

"That's the best idea you've ever had."

"Besides, he's still with Angelica."

Angelica. She's every guy's wet dream. Only problem is, if you're a guy with Angelica, then you do as she does and that happens to be every kind of illegal substance she can get her hands on. She's always been the go-to girl for parties and she wears her reputation like a cheetah wears spots. For obvious reasons, like turning her brother into a junky, Rainy doesn't like Angelica much.

The computer announces the arrival of comprehension by beeping. Rainy picks up the laptop. "Are you ready to see your prince charming?"

I stand behind her and wait for the unveiling of my next nightmare blind date. If he's anything like the last guy Rainy set me up with, he'll be a total dog. "So, what's this guy's name again?"

"Evan Laverne."

The computer flashes several pictures, all strangers to me. With a tap of the mouse pad, one picture expands to fill the entire screen. He's actually pretty cute.

"That can't be him. It's probably a fake picture or something. Don't guys online usually look...how should I put this? Dorky? Or insane?" I ask.

"Shut up!" She snaps around to hit me. "I happen to go out with guys that I meet online and no, they don't all look dorky. And very few of them look insane. Some of them, well, the ones I go out with, are freakin' hot."

"Ha!"

"You don't even know because you are too high and mighty to meet any of them."

"What-e-v-e-r. I'm not high and mighty. I just don't go around throwing myself at complete strangers." I sit back down in the blue chair. "I have standards."

People that I meet need to have something about them—a spark, a sense of intelligence, or something else to make me want to hang out with them. Rainy falls into the spark category.

"Are you talking about standards like the stupid lady in the fancy old car again? What's that name you made up for her? Ms. Lightheart?" she asks. "That's just crazy dreaming. You were what, twelve when you saw her? I think most of that occurred in your head. Nobody has a completely carefree life. Nobody is happy all the time. You just saw her on a good day. I'm sure she lives in the same hell as the rest of us."

"Oh, great, aren't you the supportive friend?" I spin away from her. "It's not her that I set my standards to. It's the principle. What's so wrong with having standards anyway? What's so wrong with having goals?"

***

I fell in love with Ms. Lightheart the first and only time that she drove through my life. Well, not love in the sense of goo-goo eyes, heart palpations, or candy-coated-lip-kisses, but love in the sense of, "Man, I totally want to be like her when I grow up."

That day, I waited for ever-late-Rainy in the park. The crisp air stung my nose and the sun swaggered low to the ground. Annoying brats just released from their own institutionalized hell, crowded the merry-go-round, the slide, and monkey bars.

That's when the epitome of what I want to be drove by. With her strawberry hair pulled back in a dancing yellow scarf, she seemed carefree, like a small girl gliding high on the swings of life. If the traffic light hadn't turned red, forcing her to stop, I wouldn't have had the chance to appreciate her from afar.

I may have fallen in love with her car first—a cream colored 1954 MG TF Convertible Roadster. Of course I didn't know what kind of car it was at the time. I only knew that when I grew up, I wanted one just like it. And when I grew up, I wanted to be her. I wanted her ivory skin hands, her long sleeve t-shirt and puffy vest. I wanted her red hair that reflected gold in the sunlight. I wanted her awesome vintage sun glasses, her car, and her fluffy sheep dog that sat in the passenger seat smiling with his tongue flapped out. Most of all, I wanted her freedom.

Her image burned into my mind that day. It's what I strive for in everyday life—perfected, carefree freedom. Four years I have attempted to live carefree, and failed. Eventually, I'll get it right. And I'll be just like her when I do.

Just like Ms. Lightheart.

***

Rainy continues to fiddle with her computer. "What? Did you say something?"

"You're such a dork." I laugh and throw a wad of crumpled paper at her.

She catches it one handed. "Yeah, but I'm a fast dork."

Pounding rattles the front door and a man's voice says, "Hey! Is someone in there?"

I freeze. Rainy mouths the words "Oh-my-God" and puts a finger to her lips.

Duh. Like I would say anything.

"Girls! I know you're in there," he shouts. "Open the door."

Sweat pricks my top lip. I mouth, "Let's go," toward Rainy and point to the back exit. She nods in agreement. We gather our things and tip-toe to the sliding glass door.

Just as I reach for the handle, a tall man in black steps to the glass. He bears a knife in his hand and a menacing grimace on his face.

Dear Jesus, help us!

If you enjoyed this sample, Dream Smashers is available for purchase on many online book retailers.

9445855R0016

Made in the USA
Charleston, SC
14 September 2011